Rick Howell

CARESSING
ISIS

A love chronicle

Copyright © 2014 by Rick Howell
First Edition – August 2014

ISBN
978-1-4602-4780-8 (Hardcover)
978-1-4602-4781-5 (Paperback)
978-1-4602-4782-2 (eBook)

All rights reserved.

No part of this publication may be reproduced in any form, or by any means, electronic or mechanical, including photocopying, recording, or any information browsing, storage, or retrieval system, without permission in writing from the publisher.

This is a work of fiction. Most names, characters, businesses, places, events and incidents are either the products of the author's imagination or used in a fictitious manner. Although some of the incidents have been created from actual events, names have been changed to protect the privacy of individuals.

Produced by:

FriesenPress
Suite 300 – 852 Fort Street
Victoria, BC, Canada V8W 1H8

www.friesenpress.com

Distributed to the trade by The Ingram Book Company

ACKNOWLEDGMENTS

Thanks to long time friend, Greg Roberts, for his reading, insightful observations and suggestions.

Photography work for the cover of this novel comes from David Harris, friend and former colleague in Japan.

To my wife Julie, editor extraordinaire, thank you for encouraging the completion of this project. You remain the Isis of my inspiration.

1980 - PROLOGUE

WAYNE Lacombe is on the phone - calling out from somewhere. In deep sensuous tones he penetrates the vacuum of twelve silent years, reaching out from the past, warping time and defying the laws of chronology. He is straining to reconnect with Jake Wilson, his old high school buddy.

"I just bought a copy of Simon and Garfunkle's Greatest Hits."

This remark is so casual, he could have just parted from Jake two hours before on the corner of Mason and View below the high school parking lot.

"I was thinking of you and the summer of '68."

Lacombe's mind is a jukebox programmed with the hits of the 60's and 70's. Name any song and Wayne will immediately assign a date and an event. "Barbara Anne", summer of '66 - timber cruising with his dad, north of Kaslo; "To Sir With Love", winter of '70-skiing with Laura at Big White; "Love is Blue" summer of '71-canoeing the Maurice with Phil Mowatt. It seems that in Wayne's mind, Jake is musically linked to the summer of '68 and particularly the "Sounds of Silence". The two graduates had one hell of a time that summer.

Wayne had this knack, this ability to read a situation, or a person, in a split second and then act directly without hesitation. Like magic, even under fire, he could produce an answer, find a solution, and discover a way out or a way in. Whatever the crisis, his face beamed with a grin that melted away the tension and worry in all those he confronted. For Jake and the other jellyfish adolescents, Wayne was a rock of certainty in their midst. Whether it was going into a bar under age or meeting some girls for the first time, Wayne oozed confidence and control. And always that grin. "Good looking boy", Jake's mother used to say and she was never wrong.

In June 1968, after they graduated, they made a couple of promises. First, they would hike the Chilkoot trail and canoe the gold miner's route along the Yukon River to Dawson City. Their Canadian History class with Mr. Bryson had them pumped and the logistics of the northern expedition had already been worked out, including the canoe rental in Whitehorse. But something happened after the summer of 1968 and the dream of gold never materialized; Wayne slipped out of Jake's radar soon after they went their separate ways to university.

Their second promise was to make every weekend of the summer of '68 an adventure. That meant they would abstain from lying on the beach with the local honeys. They would not let the summer slip away like suntan lotion on Denise Cortrell's semi-clad torso...or would they? After all, Denise Cortrell was the police chief's daughter and it paid to spend a little time with the police chief's daughter in a small town like theirs. Besides, Denise did a lot for Coppertone. On those weekends that they didn't massage lotion into Denise's body, Wayne and Jake drove the back roads of the Kootenays, inner tubed the Slocan River, rafted the Salmo and froze their butts on the peaks of Kokanee Glacier.

They packed a beat up songbook with them everywhere they travelled, a compilation of oldies, folkies, musicals and, yes, Simon and Garfunkle. Jake bought a cheap guitar and reduced every song to three chords. And they would sing the hits late into the night on the back porch or in some campground overlooking the Columbia River. But when they were on the road, the car radio would be tuned to CKLG - 730 on your dial- "good time summer radio".

"I'm playing the recording right now. Can you hear it?"

Jake imagines the receiver being pulled away from that wide grin as the faint strains of "Big Bright Green Pleasure Machine" wail from the past. And it's the summer of '68 all over again.

They're sponging their way up the Slocan Valley in Wayne's metallic green Falcon that he bought from a Doukhobor out at Crestova. It was Wayne who observed that Doukhobors only drove red and green vehicles, a mystery that could not be explained. The car was a classic, white interior with red stripes on the upholstery, bullet shaped lug nuts and a muffler that sounded like one long droning fart. Sluggish as hell until they filled it up with airplane gas at the Johnston brothers' place during one of their marathon weekend road trips. It went like stink, so fast the metallic paint started to peel on the bonnet. The car, previously beige, had been hand painted. Doukhobors didn't like beige. They didn't like clothes either.

That was the summer of yet another wave of Sons of Freedom protest marches. The whole Russian community was up in arms and down to its birthday suit. Dozens of women would strip to their balloon bottoms and walk the distance from the bus depot to the courthouse waving placards and big breasts. It was all Chief Cortrell could do with his small force of men to herd them into the chestnut trees next to the Queens Hotel before the tourists could take too many pictures.

Wayne would be there like an interviewer from CBC radio, talking with them, questioning them regarding their motives and finally asking why their daughters hadn't joined them on the march. For the most part he received only dull stares and four letter words from the Chief.

In the weeks to come these Freedomites would burn down their houses in a fiery outcry against materialism, government intervention and the jailing of their husbands. Later they would march the five hundred miles to the coast where their men were being held behind bars. Before they left they would phone the telephone company where Jake worked that summer and request a repairman to remove their set. Sometimes B.C. Tel didn't get there on time and would only find a handset sitting on an empty forty-five gallon gas drum next to a pile of charred rubble.

"I'm living on Vancouver Island now."

The tune changes from "Pleasure Machine" to "the leaves that are green turn to brown/ and they wither in the wind and they crumble in your hand".

Jake remembers humming along with his brown arm out the window of the Falcon holding on to an inner tube that is too large to put in the back seat. Wayne drives that sucker to the headwaters of the Slocan, where they toss their tubes in below the bridge and slip away into the warm current, ten miles of rapids, pools and sandy beaches. They round a corner to discover a whole commune of hippies bathing next to their tent city on the bank of the river.

Droves of them had arrived the summer before, escapees from urban America: professional people, lawyers, engineers, corporation executives, artists and the odd draft dodger. Soon the valley would become a patchwork of geodesic domes, but for now they lived in tents. Several members of the group would work outside the commune while the remainder tilled the land and produced crafts. By the time Wayne and Jake had left the Kootenays, the foreigners had established their own publishing house and theatre company.

A few waves from bodies more appealing than the big thighed women at the court house encourages Wayne to beach their tubes, cut back overland and make a second pass. Wayne drifts his tube right into the middle of some buxom maidens and by the time he has rejoined the main stream he's landed two dates for a dance at the Thrums Hall.

Wayne and Jake never make it to the confluence of the Slocan and the Kootenay but get snagged up in some log jam on a tight bend, lose their tubes and damn near their lives and have to walk barefoot to the nearest farmhouse for assistance. The residents are Doukhobor; their house is still standing and they offer the young men a bowl of borscht and a slice of fresh bread.

Wayne and Jake arrive at the Thrums Hall about 9:30 but the valley girls don't show. Wayne's been packing a condom around in his wallet all summer and is really pissed off until he spies Denise off in the corner talking to some guys in the "Thin Red Line", a local rock band. She has the Chief's station wagon and a case of beer. A grin slowly forms somewhere under Wayne's ears which slides to his jaw and breaks into a full faced crescent.

"So Jake, how've you been?"

The grin trickles out of the phone receiver, lacking something in its original magnetism. Simon and Garfunkle's "I am a Rock" can be heard in the foggy distance, lost in the wires that separate them, lost in the dashboard of the green Falcon as they speed towards Nelway.

Nelway is the US border crossing where they will have to bluff the custom officials with false statements of declaration. The new tires on the Falcon still have the stickers across the tread. Both Wayne and Jake each wear layers of new outfits purchased in the States: three shirts, a swimming suit, two pairs of pants, new shoes, a watch and a winter jacket. It's August 2nd. In the spare tire boot, a case of Hamms in a can has been conveniently hidden. They've been to Idaho where the drinking age is eighteen. They have chosen the back roads heading for Nelway, a minor crossing, hoping to avoid unnecessary suspicion.

Jake is scared shitless; Wayne is calm, whistling along with the radio. "I build walls, a fortress steep and mighty." At the dimly lit crossing the customs guy doesn't say squat so they laugh and joke their way down the Remak mining road and past the purple hotel with the yellow daisies, where in two weeks they will plunge into the icy waters of the Salmo River to chase their cedar raft towards the finish line of a six mile race.

"I am a rock, I am an Island".

"I have a daughter, Erin. She is in grade three," Wayne declares.

"I have a daughter too. She's in grade one, loves ballet and gymnastics."

"My daughter used to dance. Now she plays piano. I hope she stays with it."

The old confidence seems to ebb from Wayne's voice like air from the inner tubes they so often hunted down in the alley behind the OK Tire Shop and patched and repatched hoping they would hold until they got off the river.

"Richard Cory" begins to pulsate in the background.

"How's your wife?" Wayne wheezes almost out of breath.

"Terrific. She's as busy as ever. Loves to hike, camp and canoe - a real adventurer…"voyageur" even."

Jake recalls the fur trading adventurers from Bryson's Canadian History course they managed to survive together in eleventh grade.

"She's out with Susan, our little girl, at a mother and daughter banquet."

"I curse the life I'm living and I curse my family, and I wish that I could beeeee… Richard Cory." The recording continues until the guitar winds down in a bass spiral that finally dies in a cymbal crash.

And there's a crash in Jake's basement bedroom early one morning and his older sister's terrified voice awakens the family. She stumbles into the hall, hair in pink curlers, screaming, "There's a burglar climbing through the window." Inside Jake's bedroom, which for some unknown reason his sister automatically occupied whenever she came to visit, stands Wayne, with a grin the size of a horseshoe, chuckling as if he's just diddled Denise Cortrell in the rec room under the Chief's study.

Wayne got a kick out of watching people react to the unexpected. Sometimes he would "con" people for days on end, passing himself off as a timber baron, ski instructor, or hotel operator and to look at him, solid in the conviction of his disguises, one could not help but believe. You wanted to believe; you wanted to be connected to that assurance and to play a role in that charade.

The charade continued, Jake had learned from a mutual friend, until Wayne met his wife, Laura. Forced to drop out of college because of an unplanned pregnancy, he went to work full time for a construction firm.

Greatest Hits whines, "one man's ceiling is another man's floooor". A melancholy clarinet descends into the lower register sniffing out the corners, looking for the remains of a previous occupant and Wayne is there hanging on a thin thread way out and down - dangling - dangling on the end of a wire twelve years long.

"I've just separated from my wife."

His words struggle down the wire hesitantly, waiting for a reaction, prepared to retreat at the slightest confrontation. The grin has dried up; the confidence crippled.

"Laura has taken Erin back to the interior… to be closer to her parents. I'm here, living in a basement suite for the time being. I'm between jobs. Looking for a new start somewhere. Need to get myself together."

There is a long pause. Jake mumbles something incoherent, yet sympathetic. He is recalling the collapse of Wayne's parents' marriage and the nights Wayne would share meals with his family, sleeping over when the tension was too bitter even for Wayne's carefree nature. Those nights in the rec room revealed another side to the Wayne persona. It's that lost, abandoned voice Jake is listening to now.

The pause continues, broken by Wayne's request.

"Remember that old songbook from the summer of '68. I've lost mine in all this mess. Anyway…could you send me a copy of yours? No rush."

"Are you goin' to Scarborough Fair" filters through the condenser and mixes with Wayne's good byes…"remember me to one who lives there"…and the phone goes dead, leaving Jake in silence.

1981 - WATER WORKS

WAYNE Lacombe, the resident pool bum, leans back on the plastic chair that rests beside the steam room shower and surveys the horizon...in search of his next conquest.

He catches the eye of Tracey, a shapely lifeguard, just one in a string of women he has wooed and bedded since his wife left him last year. Tracey refuses to acknowledge his leer, quickly turns her back on his triumphant smile and takes three steps to the top of the lifeguard chair.

She is still in anguish over her short-lived affair with Wayne, a tempestuous rollick that ended two months ago. Their relationship had a promising beginning, she recalls. Wayne, the perfect gentleman, appeared at first to be kind and considerate. There seemed to be a sensitive side to his nature as well. He showed genuine interest in the woman she wanted to be and in the dreams she pursued. But when her clothes finally came off, he quickly degenerated into a jerk, leaving her soon after for a buxom waitress at the All Night Diner.

Her painful reverie is broken by a group of small boys who kick wildly behind a pink foam mattress heading for the fountain of spray that spews erratically from a giraffe neck nozzle. She hopes they are all swimmers. She completes a visual check of the pool complex. A pod of seniors lounge in the hot tub, having just completed a rigorous aquafit session. The lap lanes are full and for a moment she follows the multi coloured swimming caps as they cut through the water. She adjusts the fanny pack around her waist and picks lint from her royal blue T-shirt uniform; a green frog grins from her back letting everyone know she is a lifeguard. As a single mom she has little time to check all the laundry pockets for Kleenex and now her uniform is flecked with its remains.

The boys with the mattress are yelling at their less than attentive father whose eyes have zeroed in on a bikini-clad torso emerging from the hot tub. Sherry, the charge hand on the shift, wanders along side Tracey's chair and looks up.

"That's Janice Vickers. Her boyfriend bought her a boob job for her birthday last month."

"No kidding! He actually paid for larger breasts."

"Yeah, some guys will do anything for more than a handful."

Janice Vickers struts her stuff to the landing that leads to the water slide, checking periodically to see that everything up top is under wraps while at the same time pulling her orange suit down over her butt cheeks. Her boy friend, Jason, follows, more than aware of the visual attention his girl friend is attracting from pool patrons of both genders.

Wayne Lacombe rises from his perch and saunters closer to examine these unfamiliar mounds of flesh. He is awakened to the chase. Janice flashes him a smile as she brushes past him heading for the slides.

"Hey, Janice let's hit the steam room."

"Not yet, Jason, I want to try the slides."

Two seniors remaining in the hot tub shake their white heads, climb out and amble towards the cold showers, amazed that a bikini cup could hold so much without bursting. This will make a great story at Bridge tonight.

At the top of the slide platform, Simon, the newest lifeguard, follows the bouncing bikini top all the way up the stairs while failing to notice the T-shirt worn by its companion - until the last minute.

"Ah...Sorry, you can't go down the slide with a T-shirt on, sir. Loose clothing may get caught up on the rivet heads in the slide tunnel."

"Listen, dick head, I'm not supposed to take this T-shirt off. Your pool boss thinks my tattoos are too gross to be seen in public, so I'm forced to wear this friggin shirt. Get it!!"

Simon struggles with this unexpected information and fumbles for a response. Janice looks him up and down, inhales to expand her chest and smiles. He crumbles.

"Oh, I understand, Jason. I guess this time it will be okay."

He hopes Sherry, his supervisor, isn't watching him from her office next to the lifeguard chair.

Tracey adjusts her seating to check on the wheel chair patron who is lowering herself into the water. Wayne pops his head up from under water in the next lane and gives her a casual wave. She forces a weak smile in return.

"Hey Tracey. Got any plans for Saturday night? Maybe dinner and a movie?"

She is back in his basement suite. They have had a few beers and a vampire flick punctuates the darkness with flashes of light while Wayne fingers her buttons, snaps and zippers, struggling to expose warm flesh on which to feed. She is excited and repulsed at the same time. Her buttons pop, her snaps unhinge and her zippers part. She joins the list of the undead.

"Get lost, Wayne, Its over!"

Several more young children arrive, one obviously diapered, and race towards the water. Tracey gives the hand signal for "walk don't run" and checks to see that they have an adult with them. A mother exits the family change room and adjusts her bathing cap while listening to Sherry's reminder that children under seven need to be within arm's length of an adult.

Under the close scrutiny of Wayne Lacombe, the mother slowly descends the ladder into the pool and places her goggles over her head; she knows how to fill a bathing suit he observes but what of her status. Married? Divorced? Available? He moves closer checking her wedding finger, then looks up at Tracey with an innocent grin and another brief wave.

Tracey spins in her seat and settles her eyes on the chute at the bottom of the water slides. There seems to be some problem. A young child is standing in the tube looking back up the descent, apparently awaiting someone. That "someone" is being held back by an uncertain Simon at the top of the tube.

"I'm sorry Ma'am I can't let you go down. There's a child at the bottom trying to walk up the tube. I can see her in the video monitor."

"That is my child and she is looking for me. We started to go down together but she slipped away from me as I was sitting down. She's scared. I need to go down and reassure her that everything is all right.

"But Ma'am, you can't go down. You will collide with her and have an accident."

"Well, what do you suggest I do, lifeguard!"

Simon did not cover this scenario in his brief training session the week before. He goes into a catatonic response mode, waiting for someone more superior to take charge. And take charge they do. Tracey signals to Grace who relays the sign to Lou who jumps into the pool, reaches up into the tube and cradles the child to the landing.

"How did that happen?" queries Sherry at the break.

"I'm not sure," replies Simon. "It all happened so fast."

After changing, Lou replaces Tracey in the chair as the buzzer sounds for the wave action to begin. Amidst shrills and shrieks the powerful jet pumps cut in and the undulations begin, slow at first then gaining in frequency. The children on the foam rise on the crests and drop into the troughs struggling to stay afloat. Their Dad is nowhere in sight...but is soon picked out by Sherry's sharp eyes tossing balls with Wayne Lacombe and a group of jocks who are a regular irritation to staff. Old high school buds, which never grew up, she decides. The balls periodically skim across the waves, out of the pool and on to the deck. Tracey is kept busy retrieving the errant projectiles until Sherry reminds her that shagging balls is not her job.

Jason directs Janice into the steam room, his right hand resting on her smooth butt cheeks. Wayne Lacombe also slips inside the steam room, tired of throwing balls in Tracey's court. He sits across from Janice watching her breasts rise and fall with each laboured breath. The temperature inside the steam room is excessive. Jason punches the red knob and a surge of steam descends from above, plunging the room into a humid mist. Wayne imagines Janice dropping her top to reveal the bountiful treasures that lie beneath. Wayne has witnessed this and more in the steam room, has even been the fondler on one occasion. What was her name? Rayanne, a woman from the mainland, here for a weekend on the slopes and a little après ski action. His eyes now strain to penetrate the steamy clouds that surround the semi-naked torso before him.

Simon has closed the water slide as directed and now takes up his guarding position beside the narrow river that is separated from the main pool by an elevated island. This is a major bottleneck during wave time, the wreck of many a swimmer becoming marooned on the small island. Simon is there to give directions and a helping hand if needed. He is nervous; the mother with the tube-climbing child clinging to her neck is just entering the mouth of the river. Simon leans over the railing with a half-hearted warning that the waves are unpredictable once inside the river channel. The mother waves and continues on.

Across the pool one brave youngster is attempting to stand on the foam mattress and rides the waves like a surfer. Tracey's immediate response, the hand across the throat signal, drops the boy in mid wave and he clambers back into the water. His fellow bathers laugh and mouth, "I told you".

The tube climber has now shinnied up onto her mother's shoulders and is beginning to cry. Simon readies himself but for what he doesn't exactly know. He keeps reminding himself that he is on probation and can't afford another slip up. The well-built mother in the bathing cap, a child on each hip is proceeding up the opposite side of the river. A collision seems imminent.

Tracey checks the steam room, as part of her on deck patrol. She can barely make out the two bodies in the humid vapor but soon realizes there's more than just steaming going on between the girl with the boob job and her boyfriend.

"Ten minutes maximum in here you two. Time to move out."

A pair of hands squeezes her shoulders from behind, a firm massage grip that feels good until she recognizes the hands and whom they belong to. She turns around to face Wayne's perpetual grin, perspiration running off his chiseled jaw.

"You just don't get it do you! Keep your goddamned hands to yourself! I'm not some air head bimbo who wants to be man handled by some lowlife loser."

With a little help from Jason, Janice has slipped her bikini top back over her breasts and gives one final check to her straps. She gives Wayne an encouraging smile, grabs Jason's hand and exits the steam room. Wayne follows closely behind. All three slip into the water at the deep end of the wave pool.

Tracey stands alone in the fog, amazed at her courage. She has wanted to say this to Wayne Lacombe for two months. A sharp wrap on the glass door comes from Sherry who needs her back on deck.

The boys on the pink foam are taking turns hiding under the slab, holding their breaths and trying to push up the foam with their heads. Tracey cautions them once again about safety in the pool while glancing at the three steamers joking in the deep water.

It is about this time that floating turds are noticed mid pool.

It is Grace who makes first visual contact and quickly communicates the signal to Sherry. There is no authorized sign for human waste in the pool so Grace improvises - a quick bend, a finger to the derriere - a nasal squeeze followed by floating a single finger in the air.

Sherry is quick to read the charade and moves to the microphone announcing the need to clear the pool while Tracey automatically reaches for the emergency button that quells the wave machine.

Disgruntled children move to the exit ladders as the waves slowly subside. Janice and her boyfriend remain huddled in a corner at the deep end. Max, the maintenance man, soon appears with a net on a long pole.

Sherry surveys the pool and orders Simon to talk with the couple who still shows no signs of leaving the water. They are interlocked, clinging face-to-face, oblivious to the emergency.

The mother in the bathing cap steps forward and speaks to the maintenance man.

"Please give me the net. I'm so embarrassed. It's one of my children. I should clean it up."

"That's all right, ma'am. Just take your child to the washroom and I'll handle the rest."

Simon stands above Janice at the far end of the pool - looking and listening - perhaps more of the former, a slow flush rising from his neck into his cheeks. He turns and starts a timid walk back to his supervisor.

"What is it now?" thinks Sherry, just as Max fishes an orange bikini top from the bottom of the pool.

Wayne Lacombe smiles from the chair by the steam room door. Janice Vickers will be next.

1982 - WAYNE IN A MANGER

'TIS the season to be jolly and Wayne Lacombe is trying his best to recapture some of the joy he remembers of this festive holiday. He is hoping that Mary, his latest candy cane, will finally bring him some peace and happiness in the face of the cruel weather he has endured this past year. He is drawn to her sweet aroma and the promise of sticky encounters. So far he has managed to remove Mary's translucent cellophane and enjoy a few licks here and there but has yet to taste the full body of her stripes. Over Sunday dinner, a weekly tradition with his landlords, Ted and Jean Dawson, Wayne describes Mary.

"Warm and comforting. She smells just like Christmas baking."

"So when can we meet her, Wayne?"

"Well, she's rather busy with her singing group, 'Excelsis Deo'. Especially at this time of year with all her rehearsals and concerts."

"Oh, she's musical, is she?"

"Isn't Excelsis the group that sings at the Baptist Church, Ted?"

"I believe so. That's Pastor Russell's group. What does she sing?"

"Really high stuff by the sounds of it. I've only heard her sing a few times."

Wayne hasn't really been listening to her voice but rather watching her chest rise and fall whenever she reaches for the high notes. She told Wayne later that she had a well-developed diaphragm. Wayne misunderstood and the evening had ended in disappointment.

"So, will you be going to any of her concerts, Wayne?"

"Ah, not really, there is a carol sing through the neighborhood on Sunday night, though. Mary wants me to join in."

"Well, I think you should. It will be good for you to hang out with some church people for a change. You never know what blessings may come from it."

There is a slight drizzle when they set off from the Central Baptist Church with Pastor Russ in the lead. The plan is to make their way down the hill to the living nativity that has been set up in Resurrection Park. There they will sing carols while the story of Jesus unfolds in a manger complete with animals and angels.

Wayne is hoping the story doesn't run too long. He longs to get Mary back to his place to explore what's under the layers of scarves that drape her body. Hallelujah!

Wayne's not a trained singer but has a reasonable voice and even enjoys singing when the mood is right. He carries a few beers in his jacket pockets to ensure the mood will be conducive to holding forth "in fields as they lay". He even attempts some harmony on the chorus of traditional carols. Half way down the hill he joins with force the male Wenceslas lines "Hither page and stand by me" pulling Mary tight to his body smelling the sweet ambrosia that rises from her breasts. Mary loves her perfumes and sprays with abandon every fold and crevice. The candy cane metaphor is not without substance. Wayne wonders if she is an aficionado of flavoured lubricants as well.

"Oh! Oh! Star of wonder, star of night. Star with royal beauty bright."

Wayne holds the flashlight in one hand and a beer in the other. Mary raises the sheet of music to the light as Mr. and Mrs. Jefferson emerge onto their front porch. Zillions of megawatts radiate from every shrub, tree and bush that populate their front yard, not to mention the pulsating bulbs that run the roof line on up to the chimney. Mary, too, radiates under the lights and Wayne imagines her fronting the strippers at the local bar, undulating to the red and blue flashing backdrop, dropping scarves as the music builds.

While Pastor Russ gives a small blessing to the beaming Jeffersons, Wayne turns to follow Mary down the driveway, trips over a reindeer and lands in some dog manure. He bellows the first word that comes to mind but the choir overrides his profanity with: "Shi…"

"It came upon a midnight clear."

Mr. and Mrs. Knight have prepared a cranberry punch and serve the choir in paper cups while being crooned with "God rest yet merry gentlemen". Wayne adds some beer to Mary's cup and his own.

"O tidings of comfort and joy" echo in the garage and Wayne feels a warm glow in his toes and fingers. Mary is breathing into his neck, "comfort and joy, comfort and joy".

By the time they reach the bottom of the hill Wayne has managed to thrust a hand in between the buttons of Mary's overstuffed jacket and fumbles for a squeeze of warm flesh. At the park gate Pastor Russ reviews the order of events in the nativity story. Mary giggles as Wayne's cold hand breaks through to skin and slowly proceeds south, "following yonder star."

"Are you listening, Mary?"

Pastor Russ is concerned about his own star for this year's pageant. Mary has been somewhat distracted since leaving the Church.

"Yes, Pastor Russ. I'm listening and I'm ready to play the virgin with everything I've got."

Wayne's hand withdraws in a shot, paralyzed by the mere mention of "virgin".

"You're playing what?"

"I'm going to be Mary this year. I've been looking forward to it all month."

"You're going to be Mary, the mother of Jesus. You're going to be in the manger with Joseph and some baby tonight, standing around with a pack of animals and a Mona Lisa smile. Jesus Mary, I thought we could go back to my place, drink hot rum and lick candy canes."

"I'm sorry Wayne but this is something I have to do. You could be in the pageant too if you want. They still need a few shepherds."

And so it comes to pass, Wayne finds himself draped in a long ragged caftan and a headscarf. Someone thrusts a crook into his hand and asks him to help unload the animals.

A bearded gentleman farmer, a fusion of Noah and Old MacDonald, has delivered a truck load of animals to the park and is now herding them down a ramp off the back of his tail gate: a donkey, three sheep, a goat, a calf and sundry fowl in cages.

Wayne is given charge of the sheep, tethered together with a rope.

"Whatever you do, do not let go of this rope. These sheep have a tendency to wander and who knows what they might do in a crowd."

The park gazebo has been decorated to resemble a barn; hay bales create levels for the performers and some evergreen boughs tastefully hang from posts. A space heater has been placed in the rear to warm the holy family.

Wayne shuffles closer to Mary, clothed now in pale blue. She still radiates and must have re-perfumed, for he detects strong waves of heaven emanating from her mantle. Closer he draws, pulling the sheep with him.

"Shepherd!" shouts Pastor Russ, "Shepherds want to be close to the Christ Child; they feel a magnetic pull to his divinity. They have come to worship at his feet. Shepherds have not come to fondle the Virgin Mary."

There is a chuckle from the rest of the singers.

Wayne retreats to the crib and dutifully bends down to see the baby. He is not in a worshipping mood. He would rather be paying homage to the mother with seasonal libations.

There is no baby in the crib. Instead, a small lamb lies anchored to the floor looking at him with mournful eyes.

"We must remember the symbolic nature of the lamb," lectures Pastor Russ. "Christ is the Lamb of God, sent to forgive our sins. We are all sheep in the flock of the Lord. In this lamb lies the future of mankind. At this season of the year we look to the innocence of the lamb to set us free."

Wayne fails to see any hope in the eyes of this terrified creature lying in the manger. He hopes the poor beast has been drugged.

Someone has erected a spotlight on top of the farm truck and adjusts the beam to illuminate Mary, Joseph and the Lamb of God. Wayne kneels in its periphery, sheep turds at his feet. A second larger truck arrives and three llamas emerge, necks bobbing and twisting while they are led behind a small hillside from which the wise men will make their grand entrance.

Wayne has settled into his role (helped by another beer) as the first observers arrive and by the time the choir breaks into "O Little Town of Bethlehem", a small crowd has assembled. The rain has stopped and the clouds have parted. The temperature seems to drop. All is calm and seemingly bright, except for the small irritation growing in his bladder.

The shepherds rise and bow to the child when the angels sing "The First Noel" followed slowly by the wise men and their llamas bearing exotic packages. Throughout the drama Mary remains still and composed. Wayne is impressed but would like to see the pace increased.

It's not until Mary opens her mouth and the first notes of "O Holy Night" spill into the darkness that Wayne becomes fully engaged. He feels a warmth and a certainty filling up the manger. He senses something larger than his aimless life taking place here in Resurrection Park.

Pastor Russ speaks of the coming of the child as the coming of hope, the triumph of light over darkness.

"Each year at this time we are given another chance to start again. The arrival of the Christ child signals a fresh beginning. The baby in the manger reminds us that we do not have to continue on in the darkness anymore. We can choose to come into the light."

Wayne would love to believe this - that even *he* can step out of the darkness. But right now there is something more pressing on his mind. He wants to step into the darkness and relieve himself. He drops the rope connected to the sheep, slowly slides behind a hay bale and in the semi darkness rips open his fly.

The choir is already into the finale, "Silent Night".

"Glorious streams from heaven afar" accompanies the waterfall of three beer into the loose straw.

It's in midstream that unleashed dogs launch their attack. They first sniff and leap at the urinating Wayne who manages to beat them away with his crook. They charge into the manger where Pastor Russ is beginning his benediction.

"And now, may the peace that passeth all..."

The un-tethered sheep are the first to react to the dogs in the manger. They bolt from the gazebo, through the crowd and out of the park. The llamas spook and it's all the wise men can do to hold them to their hobbles. The calf bellows and the donkey kicks wildly at the yapping dogs who overturn the space heater that ignites the hay.

Pastor Russ and the church elders disperse the crowd and Old MacDonald withdraws his vehicles from the impending inferno. It's Mary who responds to the cries of the lamb in the manger, disconnects its tether and cradles it in her arms up onto the hillside where those who remain have assembled to watch the gazebo turn to flame.

When the fire department seems to have all under control, Wayne, Pastor Russ and Old MacDonald comb the alleys and backyards of the closest neighborhoods searching for the lost sheep. They manage to find one foraging in an overgrown garden beside a burning bush of red twinkling lights.

Pastor Russ initiates a door knocking campaign. Wayne, shepherd's robe and all, reluctantly joins in.

"Good evening. I have lost my sheep."

"Hey! Look at this, guys! Little Bo Peep has lost his sheep."

Ding Dong!

"Excuse me, I'm looking for some sheep, a pair of ewes."

"Flock off, you pervert."

Knock, Knock!

"Hello, sorry to disturb you, but have you seen a sheep this evening?"

"Oh, that sheep. We had him for dinner." A woman with a smile at the corner of welcoming lips continues, "You look tired and lost yourself, poor shepherd. Will you come in for a drink?"

The smell of homemade baking wafts from the rooms beyond. Carols play on a phonograph and voices of mirth and merriment blend with the fireplace warmth that washes over Wayne as he stands on the front porch. He is immediately transported back to his childhood. So overcome with the memory of a family he used to know, he collapses on the threshold, tears beginning to well at the corners of his eyes. He has come home. The woman at the door reaches a hand toward him and he slowly rises, longing to enter this unexpected window of joy.

"Shepherd! Rise up and follow. We have a mile to go before we rest."

The voice of Pastor Russ calls him back to the street. Wayne turns away from this heavenly refuge, thanks the woman and wishes her a Merry Christmas.

After an hour, Pastor Russ calls off the search, promising to place an announcement at the radio station in the morning. And so the three men, wise and otherwise, and a reluctant sheep, return to Resurrection Park.

All that remains of the gazebo is smoke, charred rubble and a few blackened beams. Mary is waiting for him. She embraces Wayne and a strong odor of urine and manure rises to his nostrils. She has been helping to load the animals back into the trucks and clean up the remnants of the living nativity. She is soaked and tarnished. Gone is the magic aroma that began tonight's events. Gone is the hope for soft cuddling under the mistletoe and the promise of a new tomorrow. The virgin has lost her lustre.

Wayne begs off and says good night. He saunters out of the park, still draped in the trappings of a Bedouin shepherd. He looks back to the silhouette of the stable and the outline of a woman on the hillside. In the darkness he faintly hears the opening strains of "Ave Maria".

Above, a bright star looks on.

1983 - IN THE SOUP

WAYNE Lacombe leans over a steaming pot of mulligatawny soup. He inhales deeply then stirs from the bottom the solid ingredients that Bruce, the soup man, has tossed into the mixture. Wayne is curious.
"What exactly is mulligatawny?"
"Anything I want it to be."
Bruce continues to chop this week's vegetable donations to the soup kitchen. Carrots and celery from a local farm, luncheon meat scraps from a grocery chain and a variety of spices that he has brought from home.
The potato leek concoction in the sister pot is less of a mystery and Wayne stirs the bottom residue, bringing white lumps and green ribbons to the surface.
"Sandwich time, Wayne."
A voice from down the long mid kitchen counter pulls Wayne from the revolving ripples of the post modernist painting he has churned up, reminding him of some mystical caldron where answers to the future can be unveiled.
He slides away from the stove into the realm of Thelma, the sandwich queen. He knows her name from the large tag affixed to her matronly apron. "Thelma Wilcot - St. Saviour's".
"Now this is what we do with the bread."
Thelma removes the twist tie, forces the loaf out of the plastic bag while maintaining its unity and deposits the two heels in a basin before shuffling the bread onto the counter in matching pairs. Wayne imagines her dealing cards on Bridge Night at the parish hall.
"Next, we butter one side and mustard the other."

Round slices of bologna appear and are slapped onto the mustard just before the top piece of bread seals the unit. Completed sandwiches are whisked across to Mavis, also of St. Saviour's, who quickly inserts and folds them into cellophane baggies.

"You'll find rubber gloves on the counter behind you. Always wear your gloves."

Wayne mans the mustard spreader while Thelma butters and bolognas.

"Not too much mustard, Wayne. Some of our patrons are fussy."

Behind him, Chuck and Timothy prepare wieners and buns.

"How many we doing this week, Chuck?"

"Welfare cheques went out on Tuesday so our numbers will be down, I imagine. Let's only do thirteen dozen. If we need more later, we can zap them in the microwave."

"Thirteen sounds good to me, Chuck. Too bad we have to slice the buns – It's all I could get from the bulk bread depot. What kind of wieners have we got?"

"I think they're chicken dogs, but who knows. It's a mystery."

The small talk continues. Thelma and Mavis serve on the worship committee and complain about the latest sacrilege to their traditional order of service.

"Nice of you to help us this week, Wayne."

"Oh, no problem. I'm between jobs right now so I'm available."

Wayne's not sure about revealing the real reason for his appearance here. He wonders if anyone knows that he's been ordered by the court to complete one hundred community service hours. Ted, his landlord, has suggested some of those hours could be served at the soup kitchen at St. Saviour's.

"And what do you do for a living, Wayne?"

"A little bit of everything - construction mostly. I just finished a project on Hornby Island - concrete foundation and sub floor for a high-end beach house. I didn't get the contract for the framing so now I'm looking for something else."

If the truth were known, he lost the contract because of the uptight neighbour. Half way through the job he charged him with criminal harassment and to avoid a court appearance Wayne jumped at the community service option.

"Oh that's nice Wayne - are you kind of a handy man?"

"Yeah, I guess I am."

Wayne reflects on this new label. "Handyman". How the mighty are fallen. He left high school with such ambition and promise but now lives from pay cheque to pay cheque in a basement suite. Without the kindness and concern of his landlords, Ted and Jean, he might just be a frequent visitor here at the soup kitchen himself.

"I have some chores that need doing around my place. Since my husband died last year, the house has fallen a little into disrepair. Weather stripping, porch painting, that kind of thing. Would you be interested?"

"Yeah, maybe. I could have a look at your place."

Wayne is noncommittal. He'd have to be paid under the table - so as not to skew his unemployment benefits. He's not sure if these church folks would play along with this harmless scam.

The deal is interrupted by the arrival of Lauren and Mandy. Wayne recognizes them from the pool. Mandy is handicapped in some way and Lauren is her full time aid. Wayne has watched them together tossing a ball and bouncing in the waves. Lauren is shapely, obviously fit, and watching Lauren bounce her booty in the waves was often the highlight of Wayne's pool visit. Even the bulky apron she affixes to her neck here in the kitchen cannot hide the fullness of her ample chest. Wayne smiles when she catches him eyeballing her while she ties the straps behind her back.

"Hi, I'm Wayne."

'Yes, I believe we've seen you at the pool. I'm Lauren...and this is Mandy."

"Good morning Wayne and how are you today?"

Mandy is all bubbly and wide eyed. Wayne figures she's on drugs.

"I'm fine, I guess."

"That's wonderful. Do you know what I'm doing today after soup kitchen?"

"No, I don't."

"After soup kitchen I'm going for a hair cut. And then to the pool. Lauren and I will stop at Tim Hortons for a doughnut."

"That sounds great."

"What are you doing today?"

Wayne is hesitant...a visit to his probation officer happens at 2:00 pm. This may be hard to explain...so he fakes a response.

"Well, after soup kitchen, I'm going to help Mavis with some chores at her house."

"That's nice, I'm going for a haircut - then to music lessons."

"Not today, Mandy. Music lessons are tomorrow."

"That's right, Lauren. So how are you, today, Juan?"

"I'm fine, I guess. It's Wayne."

"That's right, Wayne. Do you know what I'm doing today after soup kitchen?"

Wayne continues this dialogue around the mobius strip with Mandy until Chuck interrupts.

"So Mandy, what are you doing after soup kitchen today?"

"Good morning, Chuck. How are you today?"

Wayne edges down the counter to check out the soup once again. He slides in beside Bruce.

"So what's *her* condition?"

"She's schizophrenic - some days she doesn't say, "boo". Other days she only spouts Bible verses. We're never sure exactly who she is going to be. Just humour her, Wayne. She's doing her best."

"What do you know about Lauren? Is she single?"

"Divorced, I think? So, why are you really here?"

Wayne moves in closer and whispers.

"Community service."

"So what was your crime?"

"It's a long story. Over on Hornby Island, the neighbour used to nude sun bathe on her back patio. During coffee I would watch her with binoculars. I'm sure she knew, would give me full frontals whenever the hammering stopped. This went on for several weeks until her husband showed up at the building site while I was being entertained. He had me charged with criminal harassment.

"Oh, a peeping Tom, eh."

"Hey, I think she was bored. He works on the mainland three days a week and she tried to keep herself amused."

"I guess you were lucky. You could have been shot."

"Who was shot?"

Mandy has picked up on the last of Wayne's confession.

"No one was shot, Mandy. Wayne was saying that we need a bigger pot. The soup is boiling over."

"So who was shot, Franco?"

Lauren steps in to sidetrack the conversation.

"That's not Franco, remember, that's Bruce. He's been here making soup for three years."

"No, his name is Franco, and he's been married to my sister for twenty seven years, haven't you Franco?"

Bruce has gone silent.

"I know my own sister's husband, I should think."

Mandy has become determined. She will not let this go. Franco is in the room and he must reveal his disguise.

The whole kitchen has become uncomfortable. Bruce busies himself with chopping more onions. Lauren is gently massaging Mandy's shoulders while she rants at her would be brother in law.

Wayne throws in a life ring.

"Did you hear about the dog that was shot, Mandy?"

"I thought someone was shot."

"Yes, it was a poor dog who had been hit by a car. It had to be shot."

Thelma picks up the story.

"You wouldn't believe the number of poor dogs at the SPCA. Yesterday I walked four of them. Today I can hardly feel my arms. They just love to walk and there aren't enough walkers. Seventeen dogs at present. I can't get to all of them in a week. Remind me to take those empty bread bags, Tim. We're running short of scoopers at the kennels."

Mandy is all ears now, focused on the unravelling dog narrative.

"So who shot the dog?"

"A neighbour with a gun, I believe."

Wayne doesn't quite know where to go with the story but fears returning to the Franco episode and at Bruce's insistence he continues to reinvent.

"The neighbour was watching the street...with his binoculars and witnessed the accident...saw that the dog was in pain, grabbed his 22 rifle and marched out of his yard and put the gun to the dog's head and it was all over."

Mandy rises to the bait.

"My husband has a rifle. Keeps it behind the kitchen door - uses it to scare off crows and stray cats. The last time I was home he shot the neighbour's rabbit that had sneaked into our garden. My husband told me to lie if the neighbour came around. The next day, he showed up looking for his rabbit.

I said there were no rabbits *living* in our yard. But that's not really lying is it?"

"I suppose not, Mandy."

"The Bible is very strict about lying! The Book of Proverbs says, 'He that hideth hatred with lying lips, and he that uttered slander, is a fool.'"

Bruce shuffles uncomfortably in front of the soup.

"Here we go. Once this starts, there is no end to where we might end up."

But thankfully, Lauren is experienced with Mandy's Biblical effusions and quickly steps in to redirect the impending sermon.

"How about some tea, Mandy? I brought along some chamomile with orange spice seasoning."

"Oh that sounds delicious. Perhaps Franco would like to join us. Franco, put down your soup ladle and come into the hall for tea. I will brew you a nice hot cup of chamomile; it will soothe your nerves. I know how hard it can be living with my sister. The Bible says there is a balm in Gilead to heal the sin sick soul. I believe tea is one balm that can help to ease our pain."

Lauren guides Mandy out of the kitchen and into the hall where the kettle is kept. Bruce reluctantly follows.

Catastrophe averted, Chuck sidles up to Wayne.

"Ronald Reagan and his wife Nancy are having breakfast in the Senate cafeteria. The waitress comes over and Nancy orders her regular.

'So that will be two eggs sunny side up, coffee and wholewheat toast. And for you Mr. President?' Reagan has been studying the menu with great care and finally comes to a decision. He places the menu on his lap and looks the waitress square in the eye. 'I'll have your *quickie* easy over,' he announces.

Nancy is nonplussed and without batting an eye she calmly declares, 'Ronnie, That's *quiche*. I believe it's a *quiche* you wish to order.'"

Wayne is unsure of how one should respond to a joke like this delivered in the kitchen of St. Saviour's Anglican Church. He carefully withholds any response.

Mavis chuckles politely.

"I made a lovely quiche for the reverend last Sunday following the service. I don't think he's getting everything he needs since his wife went back to England to help her ailing mother last month. I think more of us should have him round, help to keep his spirits up."

"Well, as long as you're not having him around for a quickie, Mavis, I shouldn't imagine the worship committee would complain too much."

"Chuck, what a thing to say with the reverend in his office on the other side of that wall."

"Who do you think I heard the Reagan joke from, Mavis? At men's breakfast yesterday morning."

"Ooooh! You're pulling my leg, Chuck."

Wayne slips from the kitchen and looks for Lauren, hoping to pull her leg and perhaps something more in the bargain. She is sipping tea while Mandy sets the long tables, rolling out the plastic tablecloths.

"Hi, I'm looking for the Balm in Gilead...the balm I've never had."

A sly smile issues from behind the teacup. Enough encouragement for Wayne to continue.

"I'm a little tea pot, short and stout - here is my handle, here is my..."

"Just forget it, Wayne. I know your tune. I've heard it all before from a slew of guys just like you. Take your slick talk and refried innuendo back into the kitchen...or the gutter, if that feels more like home. I'm working right now and you have community service hours to complete."

"You know about my community service?"

"Of course, Wayne. We all do."

A shattered Wayne retreats to the kitchen. Mavis and Thelma are arranging trays as the roll top shutters are being pulled in preparation for today's clients. Timothy is chalking in the menu: Soup: potato leek, mulligatawny, Sandwiches: bologna on white and brown, hot dogs, tea and coffee.

"Should I add 'quickie'?"

"Only if you're prepared to blindfold Mavis and microwave her wiener."

"I heard that, gentlemen. Enough, and get ready for the crowd. Wayne, I'll need you to help serve at this counter. Be pleasant - ask how you can help each customer - pick up their requests and load them on a tray. Remind them that mustard, relish and catsup are on the side table, coffee and tea at the front. Any questions?"

The first half hour is brisk. Wayne listens to the homeless voices of his own community. They are a motley crew. Bathed in a fusion of urine and damp clothes, they are cheerful for the most part. Some live in the bush, some couch surf until friendships run thin while others crash in cars with expired license plates. Wayne has witnessed several of these characters in his travels. There is a hangout along the river where he kayaks in the fall. He discovers they live there year round - refusing to accept the handouts of a bureaucratic welfare state. The paper work alone, he is told, would confuse an experienced chartered accountant. Too much hassle is how they put it. Too old to hassle any more, they survive by their own wits. Wayne imagines the rebirth of the frontier spirit - urban style. Men pitted against the elements - tents and campfires, raccoon raids, scavenger bird swoops and the weekly visit by the local police.

A few are women, looking tired and wasted. Drugs he guesses. One young girl appears with a baby in her arms. He fills her order, asking her about the child, whose nostrils run caked with icicle snot. Her boyfriend has left her. Her parents have sent a bus ticket back to Alberta, but she doesn't know if she wants to leave. In the meantime she bunks with a girl friend and eats at the soup kitchen. She takes her soup and Wayne offers to hold the child while she doctors her hot dogs.

Mavis suggests that he may want to limit his contact with the clients.

"And always wear your rubber gloves. You never know what you might pick up at the soup kitchen. Last fall it was Hep C and this spring it's pneumonia."

Wayne returns to his post behind the counter. The mulligatawny is going fast, the potato leek a distant second. Many take extra sandwiches for their evening meal. At the end of lunch, left over soup will be poured into plastic containers and made available on the side table.

As mealtime comes to a close, a woman saunters into the hall through the back double doors. The light is behind her so her features are indistinguishable, yet Wayne awakens to something familiar in her silhouette. She approaches the counter, a grin beneath dark sunglasses, a confident swagger in her gait. At first Wayne fails to identify the appealing torso that stands across the counter; he has never witnessed this flesh fully clothed before.

"It's Wayne isn't it?"

"Yeah, but..."

"We haven't officially met, but I feel I know you. I'm Tania. I used to live beside that house you were building on Hornby. You probably don't recognize me without your binoculars."

"Oh, Tania...about those binoculars."

"No sweat, Wayne. My boyfriend went ape shit when he found out how you guys spent your coffee breaks. After nailing you to the wall he threw me out on my ear. So here I am. I'll have the potato leek, a hot dog and you wouldn't by chance have a place for me to stay tonight?"

1984 - VIOLINS AND VIOLENCE

WAYNE Lacombe snuggles up to his latest girlfriend, Jolene, who informs him that she is a thespian. They are sitting together in Wayne's basement suite where he hopes they will complete their first date in bed. Wayne knows that a thespian is not a lesbian, although he has been confused by the terms on occasion. He is momentarily shocked, and takes several seconds to recover from the announcement. Unsure exactly of the meaning of this tricky word, he cautiously circumvents any further discussion of "thespian", filling the silence instead with romantic innuendo involving the special ribbed condoms he has stashed in his bedside drawer.

Jolene persists, "If you truly want to understand me, Wayne, you must recognize my dramatic aspirations."

"Oh sure, I think you were made for the stage, Jo. Now would you like to see those rainbow coloured rubbers?"

"Further, Wayne, if you wish to share in the love of my body, you will first have to share in my love of the theatre."

"Of course, I'm ready to share anything you want, Jolene. I'm a real team player."

"Good. So you won't mind if I include your name in the stage crew for the upcoming little theatre production. We are presently short staffed backstage."

Wayne is caught off guard. For a moment he resists, but Jolene's sensual lips and voluptuous curves have him promising anything for just a taste of what lies beneath her tightly fitted top.

On Friday evening Wayne shows up at the Community Theatre ready to push scenery and hang lights.

The show is a one-act production of *Schubert's Last Serenade*, the local entry into the zone festival. Wayne soon discovers that Jolene plays Bebe, a snotty Ivy League university student. The leading man is a burly construction worker named Alfred, played by a burly construction worker named Reg. The two characters have collided prior to the opening scene of the play on a demolition site where Bebe is protesting the destruction of an historic building. At the same time, Alfred and his crew are tearing the building down. The two clash on the front lines resulting in Bebe's head injury and a visit to emergency.

Wayne meets the director, Trevor Walsh, a thin balding man, who promptly hands him a floor plan of the set, which reads *Elegant French Restaurant*. It is here that Bebe and Alfred meet following their showdown on the demolition site.

Downstage, several round tables, white tablecloths, and full table settings. Upstage left, a large potted palm behind which Schubert will play his violin during Alfred and Bebe's intimate dinner. Upstage centre, swinging doors that lead to the kitchen and down right, a counter, home base for the maitre d' who reads stage directions during the entire play.

With a little help from Reg and Jolene, Wayne learns about "up stage" and "down stage" - "stage left" and "stage right". Once the set pieces have been placed and approved by Trevor, Wayne is told to tape the floor to help speed things up for next Wednesday's rehearsal.

Wayne is quick to notice the easy familiarity of the cast and director. They stand with arms around each other, hands on buttocks with ample doses of cheek kissing as the remainder of the ensemble arrives.

Trevor directs Wayne to the prop table, which consists of a pile of kitchen utensils, several bottles of non-alcoholic wine, glasses, plates, cutlery and a violin. He is told to organize the table by taping labels for every item that lies in the pile. This keeps him occupied during the actor warm up and the director's opening remarks.

Wayne is more than aware of the affection Jolene is heaping on Trevor. She hangs on every word, laughing at every suggestive comment he makes - and making a few of her own when describing her motivation for meeting Alfred in the restaurant.

The rehearsal begins. Wayne is told to wait in the wings and take notes of items that are missing or set pieces that need to be adjusted and re-taped.

The play opens with Bebe sitting at the down stage table, head wrapped in a white bandage, adjusting her make-up using a small hand mirror. She applies orange lipstick to those full lips Wayne has barely tasted and he is reminded of why he is here.

Alfred enters, dressed in coveralls, hardhat and tool belt. He appears to have come directly from work. Dangling from his belt, his implements of destruction: hammer, pipe wrench, and crowbar. An argument ensues with the maitre d' regarding the removal of the hard hat in the restaurant.

During these opening lines the woman playing the waitress fumbles around the prop table searching for menus. In desperation she grabs two pieces of plywood and enters the scene with these substitute props.

"Cut, cut, cut! Where are the menus, Rachel?"

"I don't know, Trevor, they were here last rehearsal. They seem to have disappeared. They weren't on the prop table."

"Walter, Walter, I thought I told you to organize that prop table. What did you do with the menus?"

Jolene interrupts, "Trevor, his name is Wayne."

"Walter, Wayne, whatever. Where are those damn menus?"

A shy voice from the sound booth.

"Ah... Trevor, I had to take them back to the restaurant for my shift after Wednesday's rehearsal and I forgot to bring them tonight."

"Geez Louise, can't we get some menus that we can hang on to until this show is done?"

"I'm still looking for some old ones, but the boss is real bitchy these days."

"Walter. Write down menus on your list and see what you can do about getting some for next Wednesday's rehearsal. Come on folks! We only have one more week till the festival. Now let's take it from the top."

The rehearsal continues in much the same manner. Stops and starts with Wayne madly writing down missing props and readjusting masking tape on the floor.

The play ends in a long passionate kiss between Alfred and Bebe, as the maitre d' screams out counter stage directions "Alfred cracks her across the jaw. Bebe screams and rushes off".

Even Wayne gets the point of the play although Jolene lectures him on the way home in the truck.

"So you see Wayne, these two characters have been following stage directions all their lives that have been written for them by society and the different classes they come from. Bebe has been raised and trained to look down upon the common worker while Alfred has been programmed to resent and detest his so-called intellectual superiors."

Pause.

"The maitre d' is the voice of reason. The chances of these two individuals from opposite social and educational poles becoming a couple is almost impossible. Yet the play affirms the power of love over social structures."

Another pause while she inhales for the next breathy pronouncement.

"Their romance is a denial of all that they have been raised to become. Isn't that wonderful...kind of like you and me, don't you think?"

"So what's the deal between you and Trevor?"

"Trevor! Oh he's just an old friend. We've been doing theatre together since we were in university."

"Are you still sleeping with him?"

"I beg your pardon? Trevor is a professional. He's married and has two children."

"Well, you look awfully chummy to me."

"You're not jealous, are you...Walter?"

Stage laughter is followed by a kiss on the cheek with those warm succulent lips. Wayne is anxious to get home and take full advantage of Jolene's assets, dramatic and otherwise, but he is stopped after a little fondling on her back porch.

"I have an early morning, Wayne, and besides we don't want to go too far too fast, do we? Let's make it last. Think of our relationship as a script. The scriptwriter doesn't put the climax in the first scene, he slowly builds the tension, increasing the intensity of relationships as the action plays out. See you at Wednesday's rehearsal."

Wayne drives home and dreams of lips, violin bows and crowbars.

Wednesday is more of the same, except Schubert, the violinist, is in absentia. His violin sits idle on the prop table. Trevor asks Wayne to temporarily fill in for tonight's rehearsal. Reluctantly and with a little encouragement from Jolene's lips behind the swinging door, Wayne finds himself standing behind the potted palm bowing rhythmically to the sound track of Isaac Perlman, run by Louise up in the sound booth.

He adjusts his arm movement to reflect the changing tempo of the music, which in turn supports the changing dynamic of the relationship between Alfred and Bebe. He bows fiercely during a heated argument about stereotyping then fluidly during a romantic session of hand rubbing and soothing dialogue.

Wayne is almost enjoying himself. Half hidden by the palm fronds he can observe the interplay between the maitre d' and the two lovers he manipulates. At one point Schubert is required to step out from behind the palm tree and shake his violin violently at the two lovers. Jolene spreads her lips in a broad smile and adds a wink of approval.

They all stop for coffee at the "Gravel Grind" following rehearsal and review the evening's progress. Trevor is full of praise. It has been a good session. He announces that Schubert, unfortunately, has been transferred to Vancouver and will not be able to fulfil his obligations to the show.

He continues, casting his glance towards Wayne who has not been listening. He has been preoccupied with Jolene's cleavage, which opens its deep tunnel every time she leans forward to second Trevor's observations.

"Walter, I think it only fitting after tonight's trial by fire that you should be given the first shot at the role of Schubert. You certainly stepped up to the plate at short notice tonight to give us a convincing cameo of the musical maestro. What do you say?"

Wayne is caught off guard. The entire table of thespians turn to face him. Until now no one has really noticed him, other than as an appendage of Jolene. The lights seem to increase in their intensity. Wayne glows in this new warmth of recognition, delighting in this sensation that recalls the glory days of high school. He is once again the centre of attention. All eyes await his response. He opens his mouth to speak, but holds the moment a little longer, in true dramatic fashion, basking in the lime light.

"I think I could do the part," he mumbles.

Jolene is on her feet, kissing him on the mouth. Other lips are on his cheeks, welcoming him to the inner circle. He has just graduated from crew to cast and the congratulations are overwhelming. Trevor takes his hand but forgoes the shake to replace it with a hug.

Wayne, for the first time in a long time, feels part of something larger than himself. For the moment he forgets Jolene's cleavage, the exposed skin above her belt and those expansive lips. He rides home buoyed up by the recent turn of events but not before first stopping at the Community Theatre to pick up the violin. He needs to practice, he informs Jolene.

Friday is dress rehearsal. Wayne looks stunning in the tuxedo from the Salvation Army - wine tie and cummerbund particularly engaging. He and Jolene cut a fine figure in the warm up room as Trevor leads them through a series of physical and vocal exercises. Reg struggles in the warm up due to the shear weight of the tool belt and removes it to free up his body. Wayne tries it on and the cast erupts in laughter at the juxtaposition of tux and tool belt. Wayne brandishes the hammer and bows it like a violin much to the delight of his audience. These warm ups are more fun than the play, notes Wayne.

The rehearsal goes well apart from a few technical glitches, which Trevor is not too happy about.

"Now listen, techs, your role in this production is all about precision. Lighting and sound *can be* perfect. It's a simple process of accuracy and timing of "on" and "off". There is no excuse for missing a cue. Am I making myself clear?"

There is some embarrassed nodding by Louise and Jeremy, a pimply-faced young man running the lights. The actors breathe easy; their criticism will come later. But before Trevor delivers his notes to the actors, he provides the updated schedule for the festival.

"We appear first on the Friday night slate. There are nine One Act plays in total this year at the festival: three on Friday night, three on Saturday afternoon and three Saturday night. Winners will be announced following the last set of plays on the final night."

"Curtain for us is 7:30 pm, Friday. I want you back stage at 6:30 for make-up and costume. Warm Up starts at 7:00 pm."

In Jolene's kitchen, Wayne is permitted to plumb the depths of her flimsy blouse, but is stopped short of revealing his own plumbing by a back pedalling Jolene who reminds him of the thespian code of conduct.

"Wayne! Actors should not fraternize until the show is put to bed. Personal relationships between performers only compromise the quality of the production. I am saving myself for the show."

This sounds an awful lot like Trevor bullshit but Wayne lets it go for the time being. He can't believe the hoops he's had to jump through to win over this thespian.

Back stage at the festival hall, everyone is a little nervous. Wayne feels uncomfortable in his tux and even more so in the layers of cake on his face. Some Trevor look alike has been working on him for twenty minutes. Applying a sticky base, followed by highlights and shadows that make him look older than his thirty-four years. A few wrinkles and some white tinting of his hair place him in his distinguished sixties.

Jolene radiates with warm cheeks and accentuated lip lines. Even the blood-stained bandage around her head glows under the make-up lights. Wayne is encouraged that this pretence will soon be coming to its natural climax.

The warm up room is a carpeted affair with minimal chairs and a lone table, on which Reg places his loaded tool belt. Trevor takes control immediately at 7:00 pm.

"First we need to increase our energy flow, then focus on the job each of us has to do and finally slip completely into our characters before we move to the stage."

The group enters into a follow-the-leader activity with Trevor weaving his way around the room over chairs, under the table, leaping and cavorting in wild frenetic action. Wayne is pulled into the physical energy of this dance and grabs the pipe wrench from Reg's tool belt swinging it with abandon. Considering he's been drawn into this grand illusion he might as well enjoy himself in the process. Round and round the room they proceed, new leaders emerging as the dance continues. The room is now vibrating with energy as voices are added to the gyrating. Loud syllables of nonsense echo off the walls and shrieks of madness charge from the mouths of these fierce maenads.

At the height of festivity as Wayne swings the wrench violently through the air he accidentally catches an unsuspecting Jolene on the upper lip, tearing through lipstick, make-up and skin.

Immediately the energy drains from the room; a sudden stillness descends as blood spews forth from the sacrificial Bebe. It is Louise who finds a make-up towel and presses it into Jolene's mouth; ice soon follows. But the blood is unstoppable;

it seeps through the wrinkles of the towel and down Jolene's fingers that clutch the ice against her mouth.

Reg springs into action, grabs the wrench from Wayne's wobbly hand and belts the weapon securely. He crosses the room to confer with Trevor regarding the approaching curtain time only ten minutes away.

"There's no way we can do this show. Jo has the main role. You need to talk to the festival stage manager right now. No way this is going to happen. No way!"

Trevor is less hasty. He has invested a great deal into the production and does not want to bow out so quickly. He speaks tenderly to Jolene, checking on her condition.

"Jolene, if we can get you patched up, would you be willing to go on stage later tonight?"

Jolene is the consummate thespian, prepared to go all the way for her director.

"Yes", she mumbles through the towel. "The show must go on."

Trevor exits the room in search of the stage manager.

Wayne sits crumpled in the corner; never has he been so up and then so down. His soaring spirits have crash-landed leaving him spineless and deflated. He is detached from all that surrounds him and realizes that he alone has brought the roof down on this production and on Jolene's passion for the stage. He looks across the room at his object of desire, the provocative Bebe - draped in a blood soaked towel - staring at him with menacing eyes. He tries to smile weakly in return, trying to imagine those sensuous lips behind the towel.

"Walter! Walter! You need to take Jolene to Emergency immediately and get her back here by 9:30. The stage manager has moved us to the last spot this evening. All is not lost." Trevor is fully animated, locked in overdrive.

"Snap to it, Walter! Get a move on."

They bundle Jolene in a warm jacket, and lead her out to Wayne's truck. The drive to the hospital is silent. Jolene unable to talk; Wayne afraid to speak.

An hour and a half later they are backstage in a feeble attempt to warm up for their performance. Their energy, however, remains rooted in the blood stained carpet beneath their feet.

Jolene's punctured upper lip has been butterfly stitched, band-aided and coated with heavy make-up. The swelling is noticeable but she continues to apply ice until the curtain rises.

Schubert's Last Serenade is not a spirited performance. The cast is shaky but not completely broken. They manage to finish the play. Although Jolene presents a stiff upper lip at the down stage table of the elegant French restaurant, her speech is slurred and all but the front row have any idea what she is saying. The adjudicator notes that the lead actress could benefit from some voice work in order to improve articulation.

The curtain falls and the cast disappears, shrouded in gloom. Trevor reminds them that they need to be back for Saturday night's finale while helping Jolene into his car.

On Saturday, the production is recognized with two trophies: best set design and best performance of a minor role. The violinist, Schubert, played by Wayne Lacombe receives the annual "spear carrier" award.

Wayne tries to contact Jolene over the next week. She is taking no calls and refuses to answer her door.

As a final act of contrition, Wayne leaves his small, engraved trophy, the two masks of tragedy and comedy mounted on a walnut base, sitting on her back porch railing.

1985 - A WALK IN THE SUNSHINE

IT'S "Bring a Guest Day" at McDivots Golf Club, part of an early season promotional effort to increase membership at this local, nine hole course. Ted Dawson has invited his tenant, Wayne Lacombe, to join him. Wayne has been unemployed all spring, spending his days in front of the television screen watching videos that his most recent girl friend, Cassie, brings from the shop where she works. Cassie and the videos have become Wayne's anti-depressant medication this spring. He longs for a new beginning but cannot elude his past. This is the season when Wayne struggles with his demons, the aimlessness of his life and his legacy of missed opportunities.

Ted wants to pry Wayne off his butt and out into the fresh air so informs him of the guest opportunity at McDivots. Ted pictures himself as Wayne's personal rehabilitation director, so Wayne doesn't want to disappoint him by saying "no". Wayne likes Ted, in spite of his simplistic optimism. Wayne is not a golfer...well, maybe a little back in high school, but that doesn't count. Nor does he own clubs. He uses those belonging to Jean, Ted's wife, who gave up on the game shortly after Ted bought them on a whim for an anniversary present.

It's a crisp morning in early March, but the sun is shining. Ted rolls into the parking lot just before 9:00 am with Wayne at his side. The perfunctory good mornings are exchanged with others who carefully unload clubs and shoes from the trunks of their expensive import cars. Miles has a new Toyota Celica and a cluster of men in golf attire stand around the hood that Miles has raised to show off his high performance engine. There is a showroom atmosphere as Miles holds forth with statistics on pollution control and gas consumption. Several nods and plenty of envy. Everyone wonders where Miles' money comes from. Probably one of those prairie farmers come west for retirement. The club house is full of them. Ted seems to know them all and introduces Wayne as his young friend.

Behind the counter is Belle, the best thing Wayne has seen so far. She smiles a welcome to him and jokes with the senior crowd who register their foursomes on a large sheet in front of her. Wayne tries to catch her eye, wondering where he has seen her before and imagining where he might see her again. While signing in, he gives her a winning smile followed by his best opening line.

"It's Belle, isn't it," staring at the name tag on her ample chest. "Didn't we skinny dip together out at the lake when we were kids?"

Belle blushes and gives Wayne a shy grin. Her breasts swell, pushing her nipples against her blouse and Wayne envisions a wet T-shirt contest right here in the club house.

"Actually, no, but I was a high school cheerleader back when you played basketball."

Wayne is about to propose they meet for drinks later when Ted motions him away from this contest of gender posturing, the only sport he has ever mastered.

Their tee time has already been set. In the interim, ten minutes spent on the putting green is customary where more socializing occurs - mostly sports related. Wayne sinks some ten foot putts and is encouraged. He meets the other two that will join his foursome. Jock, an aging Scot, shuffles across the putting surface to shake Wayne's hand and Miles, the car salesman. As they move toward the first tee box at a snail's pace, Wayne realizes that he is here for a long time not a good time.

The course is short but picturesque. In the distance sit the glacier and surrounding mountains that Wayne knows as intimately as the crests and valleys of Cassie's topography. But it's the ups and downs that lie beneath the blouse of the fair Belle that have Wayne excited as he salutes the yellow flag on the first green with a seven iron. His first ball is pulled from the air by an invisible arm that reaches from the pond on the right, while his second ball sails over the barbed wire fence to the left.

"Tough start," quips Miles who walks alongside Wayne up the fairway, detailing the fuel efficiency of his new vehicle.

The mention of piston strokes reminds Wayne that he has already taken four strokes and is still not on the green. He over chips and takes two putts to the green for a triple bogey, which Jock announces loudly as he writes down scores on the card. Jock likes the sound of triple bogey and repeats the phrase several more times trippingly on his Scottish tongue before they reach the second tee box.

By hole number three, conversations have moved from sports to health. A litany of doctor's visits, lab reports and pending surgeries drop like geese manure, through which they weave their carts - geese winter on these fairways making the golfer's trek precarious. Miles is awaiting a hip replacement, Jock proudly pats his new pacemaker and Ted moans in a subdued voice of his enlarged prostate.

On the long par four, Jock relates how Eric, his former partner, collapsed "right over there" while fishing a ball out of the lake.

"It took three of us to carry him to the club house. He was having a great round until he hit the water," he continues. "A birdie and two pars. A massive stroke; we saved his life but he is not happy about it," he concludes.

On hole five, Ted hooks one into the trees and miraculously the ball ricochets back out onto the fairway.

"Thank you, Percy," he solemnly declares.

"Percy had a fatal heart attack here two years ago," relates Miles, as Wayne follows Ted's ball with a hard drive into the trees but without the miracle.

"I guess you didn't know Percy," says Jock, pulling a ball from his pocket and tossing it to Wayne. "Here, give it another go."

Wayne finally nails it and the ball sails two hundred yards to drop just to the left of the green.

"That'll bring you back," utters Jock.

Wayne manages to chip into the sand and then takes two strokes to extricate himself. Fortunately, he sinks a fourteen foot putt.

"That'll bring you back," says Ted.

"Another triple bogey for the young lad," registers Jock, as he lines up his putting ball on the green.

This differs from his fairway ball in that a felt pen ring circles the sphere enabling Jock to align the roll of his ball towards the hole.

"Does it work?" asks Wayne, as Jock's ball plunks into the hole.

"That'll bring you back," proclaims Miles.

Jock runs into his own grief on hole six. He duffs his tee shot, slices into the lake, over shoots his chip and lands in the trap behind the green.

"Tough hole," says Wayne with an edge of sarcasm.

"Well, you know," says Jock, and a serious tone takes hold of his shaking body. "I'd rather be here at McDivots slicing balls into the water than sitting in Mountain View Old Folks Home staring at the wall - like poor Eric's doing right now."

Wayne's been to the home - had a girlfriend who worked there once. Used to visit Natalie Fawcett late at night when the patients were asleep. She would show him how to make a bed up right and proper. Taught him everything he knows about plumping up pillows. Besides Natalie's pillow talk, Wayne recalls the wheelchair bound remnants of humanity staring with blind submission at flickering television screens.

"You should be glad you can walk in the sunshine," continues Jock. "Anything beyond that is gravy."

"I see your point," says Wayne.

Hole number seven is a short one. Wayne's eight iron shot lands six feet from the pin.

"Where did that come from?" declares Ted with a smile.

Miles, not one to compliment, describes his hole-in-one on number seven last year. "My five wood drive hit the bank over on the left there, kicking the ball onto the green. Then the ball just disappeared. Didn't realize it was a hole-in-one until we all arrived on the green. Lucky shot, I guess."

He promptly drives his ball into the tree on the left and the ball disappears, failing to drop to the ground.

"Maybe it's in the hole," jests Ted, tired of hearing Miles' hole-in-one story every time he tees up on number seven.

The ball is, in fact, wedged in the crotch of two branches. An argument ensues about a penalty stroke and continues as Wayne makes his put for a birdie. Jock is reminded by Ted to write down a "2" for Wayne.

The eighth hole passes without incident, save for Miles' missed hit off the tee that careens off of Ted's knee into a drainage ditch. Ted is brought to the ground but not before a gush of colourful nouns let fly from this mouth. For a moment Wayne imagines he is back working construction.

So unlike Ted, the group stands dumbfounded, amazed at the language spewing forth as he gathers himself together and attempts to rise. Wayne moves forward to assist but Ted waves him off.

"I'm all right, Goddamnit. Jesus, Miles. You could at least wait until I'm standing behind you. Can't a guy even tie up his shoe without being attacked? You brainless twit!"

Miles is almost apologetic but insists he can take a mulligan, because his ball has been impeded by a man-made obstacle. Ted hobbles to the tee box and dribbles a weak shot down the fairway, cursing under his breath.

"There goes my game. Dammit."

"Oh, play another ball," suggests Wayne, recognizing the need to assuage Ted's hostility, something he has never witnessed before.

"I never take mulligans," responds Ted. "Real golfers play the ball where it lies." He stares hard at Miles as Miles tees up a second ball.

The ninth fairway leads back to the club house, a small pond bordering the right flank. Wayne's tee shot is a beaut but it fades a little and ends up just in the water.

"You'll be able to find that," assures Jock. "I am a regular customer in that territory. There are more balls in that pond than condoms in the river. Did you know, the management once had a scuba diver comb that pond? He emerged with eight hundred and sixty three balls. And the management kept them all. In all decency they should have been given back to the poor suckers who drove 'em in there."

"How would they do that?" queries Wayne.

"A lot of them balls have golfers names on them, that's how! You can see them corralled in the big bin by the club house door. The JP's are mine. They want a dollar for every ball in that bin."

"Well you know," says Wayne, "lookin' at those balls in the bin has got to be better than sittin' in a wheelchair at Mountain View, watching Bob Barker."

"You bet," replies Jock with a wry smile.

Wayne pulls his cart up beside the pond and stretches out with his nine iron to cradle the ball that lies nestled in silt about a foot deep in the water. He has left his cart on a precarious angle on the side hill that falls away to the pond. Just as he is about to reclaim his ball, the cart begins a slow descent. Wayne quickly spins away from his ball to save the cart, but loses his footing and topples into the water with the cart following. The move is almost graceful, like a ballerina executing a pirouette with a leather partner.

All this is within view of the outdoor tables in front of the clubhouse. Several members rise from their coffee and walk toward the ninth green to catch the full picture of the fiasco. For some, this total baptism of the neophyte marks the highlight of their morning ritual.

The small covey of vultures advances further, preparing to witness the drama that will follow. They are all too familiar with the golfer who crosses the line of sanity and falls off the edge, succumbing to the impossibility of the game. Shattered golf clubs have been observed lying beneath trees; a five iron still hangs from the branches of an old alder on the other side of the fence on number three. A club shaft, sheared and impotent, was recently extricated from the ball wash on number seven. Golf bags periodically appear floating like abandoned corpses on the calm lake beside number four. Not all golfers explode, however, some just pick up their balls and walk a straight line to the parking lot, wordless - dejected and defeated.

And so the growing gallery advances even further to witness yet another sacrificial offering to the unforgiving gods of golf.

As Wayne wrestles with his cart and struggles to shore, the membership stands in silence. They collectively await an outburst of cosmic proportion. Secretly, they long for the collapse of this new comrade and prepare to welcome him to the community of the fallen.

But Wayne is composed, wet T-shirt clinging to his chest. He looks towards the clubhouse, smiles, places a ball on the grass and chips to within two feet of the hole.

"Are you all right?" The first to speak is Ted. "I'm impressed with your calm, Wayne."

"I'm fine," says Wayne, "never felt better, never felt younger, never felt more alive."

Ted is confused until he follows Wayne's gaze beyond the ninth green to a radiant Belle standing on the fringe, waving a cold beer towards him.

"Besides," he says, "I found seven balls while floundering around in that damn pool and three of them have JP on them."

Wayne makes his putt, parring the ninth hole, takes the beer from Belle and strides towards the locker room, his left hand clutching her right buttock.

1986 - KNIGHT ERRANT

W<small>AYNE</small> Lacombe sings baritone in the local barbershop chorus. Not many folks know he can sing and Wayne himself is surprised by the sounds that come from his mouth when surrounded by the voices of the ensemble. It is Ted, the director, who talks him into joining. As Wayne's landlord and benevolent protector, he once again assumes this unacknowledged role. After all, Wayne is almost family.

Ted and his wife, Jean, aware of Wayne's directionless life, odd hours and questionable lifestyle go out of their way to impose some order and stability to this single man's existence. They invite him for meals, offer him the fruits of their garden and generally look out for his well-being. Ted has generously forked over the money for several traffic violations and even covered the Hydro bills while Wayne has been temporarily unemployed. When not locked in the upheaval of ever-changing lady friends, Wayne struggles with financial debt.

Wayne had no desire to sing in some old guys' group until he witnessed first-hand the power these crooners have on women. On various occasions Ted and the boys perform for selective audiences: service clubs, senior's homes and romance parties. It is at one of these latter gatherings in the home of his sister that Wayne experiences the unusual effect of romantic ballads on middle-aged women. The romance party, much like the Tupperware craze of the 60's, utilizes the fabric of friendship to flog intimate products - lingerie, erotic literature, and soft-core sexual aids. To this hen party of the twenty first century, Wayne, of course, is not invited; he, instead, has been banished downstairs to baby-sit his sister's kids, which soon becomes secondary to watching the football game and consuming his sister's beer.

However, when the singing begins upstairs, Wayne is drawn, like Eurydice, from the depths into the light of barbershop harmony. And boy, can those old geezers sing. Who would think that such a hodgepodge of physical specimens could generate such a sound. And their age and deformities do not seem to hinder the profound effect they are having on their listeners. On the sofas, lounge chairs and throw cushions, women flush and melt as the quartet plays to the ladies' inner emotional sanctums. These guys have class; they pitch their songs to individual faces in the room who first squirm, then open and finally buckle into heart rendering sobs. Overcome by the words they have never heard from husbands and lovers, they become girls again, bathing in the warmth of undivided love and attention. Like ladies of a medieval court, elevated and adored, these women glow in the light of this ancient love tradition. And the guys seem to be having a good time too, Wayne notices. Several of the troubadours even leave with a gushing romantic on their arms. Wayne quickly imagines the effect he might have on the available women of the town. With the addition of a sensual voice to his athletic build and chiseled features, he could become another Don Juan.

And so Wayne decides it is time to sing. Ted, of course, is thrilled and drives Wayne to his first practice in the basement of the Catholic Church, Our Lady of Recapitulation. The smell of potluck hangs in the air, the remnants of an earlier church meeting. Posters of missionary outreach plaster the faded walls and thirteen chairs form a semicircle in the middle of the room. "The Last Supper" lies scrawled on a white board with some Bible verses duly noted underneath.

Wayne meets the barbershop disciples who seem even more peculiar, until they begin to sing. "Consider yourself one of the family!" they bellow, welcoming Wayne to the fraternity of the chorus. Ted checks out Wayne's voice range and quickly assigns him to the baritone section - one old dude and a young kid. In fact, the group seems to be composed entirely of seniors and juniors with few members in between. The maturity levels, on the other hand, are the same. Lots of wise cracks, physical jostling and wandering around the room during sectionals. Wayne feels like he is back in middle school. It is all Ted can do at times to keep the rehearsal under control. But, as soon as the singing commences, all that changes. The chorus is focused, attentive and aware of the critical balance between voices. Together they are so much more, stresses Ted, a self-taught philosopher. "The whole is greater than the sum of the parts," he continues. The rich tones seem to penetrate the entire fellowship hall, including the statue of Our Lady who virtually glows in the shadows at the far end of the room.

Wayne leaves the gathering invigorated, humming in the car all the way home. Ted beams beside him. He has rescued yet another wayward soul, he announces to Jean that evening over a glass of wine.

That was last year. Since his epiphany, Wayne's attendance at rehearsals has been intermittent and his enthusiasm has somewhat waned. After several weeks of intense practice Wayne finds out that singing baritone does not quite have the desired effect on the woman he is presently pursuing. Baritones rarely sing the melody, he discovers, and without the full composite of bass, tenor and lead, the baritone line is rather irregular, if not downright unlistenable. It jumps up and down at strange intervals, which make little sense without the accompanying parts.

Wayne first realizes this when singing outside the apartment of Jessica late one night after a brief spat. Jess quickly closes the window and pulls the drapes. Soon after, while sitting on a bench with Patricia, at Rotary Park, Wayne breaks into "My Wild Irish Rose", and Patricia rises, steps into her car and quickly squeals away. Several weeks later in the bedroom of Allison, when he hums, "What a Lovely Way to Spend an Evening," sounding much like a bassoon practicing arpeggios, Allison reaches over and turns on her bedside radio. Wayne is deflated. His ego in tatters, he questions the value of singing in a barbershop quartet if he can't serenade his latest love interest with the music of the heart - all by himself.

It is obvious that he only sounds good with the chorus beside him. How can he possibly court and conquer with three other guys continually backing him up? Romance, he always figured was something you did on your own. At night he dreams about intimate dinners with three waiters in red polo shirts helping him break down the barriers of each new lover and later in the bedroom, the same three guys in the shadows harmonizing as he fondles under the covers. He would wake from these nightmares in sweat and sing the opening bars of "Shine on Me!"

And so Wayne slowly becomes a member at large - infrequent, and uncommitted. When Wayne finds work out of town, Ted assumes the end is near.

49

And then early in October, in the middle of "Danny Boy", Wayne stages his return. Ted is at the piano chording while the rest of the chorus finds its pitch. Wayne sashays up behind Ted and declares. "How's it going old buddy?" While some of the members roll their eyes and others look at the ground and one mutters towards the statue of Our Lady in the corner, Ted turns around to face a smiling Wayne.

"Are you here to sing?" pronounces Ted - a nod from Wayne. "Then take a seat!"

At break time Wayne makes two announcements.

"I'm back," he says, apologizing for his irregular attendance and lack of commitment.

"I like you guys," he declares, "and want to be a part of this great society dedicated to the preservation and propagation of barber shop music. I promise to attend all practices and to memorize my music punctually."

"And secondly, I have found the love of my life. Her name is Olive. She lives in Williams Lake. I discovered her in the personal ads."

A voice from the back of the room, " Have you met her yet?"

"Not yet," continues Wayne, "but we talked on the phone last night. Olive arrives on Saturday and I want to bring her to barbershop next Thursday night."

More eye-rolling and a few smirks.

"And I would like to sing for her, if three of you guys would help me out. I'd like to sing the lead in 'Heart of my Heart'."

A silence...broken by Ted who suggests his request might be possible. Cecil, Bud and Raymond volunteer to help out.

"We should practice," says Wayne.

"At the end of rehearsal," counters Ted. "Right now we have music for the upcoming concert to cover."

At the next bass sectional in a side room, Bud warns the new guys against lending Wayne money. Several of the members have been burned, he informs them.

After the traditional closure to the session "Keep the whole world singing" and "It's great to be a barber shopper!" Wayne, Raymond, Cecil and Bud rehearse for the big serenade. On the last line, "Say you'll be mine forever", Wayne kneels in front of Ted's chair, offering him a pencil, in rose like fashion. Ted folds in mock tears and the rest of the chorus falls to laughing.

"I was pretending you were Olive," confesses Wayne.

"I realize that," says Ted.

"Well, I hope so," says Wayne, requesting a second run through.

Ted says he will sing along with him if he promises to get off his knees and take the pencil out of his face.

"I plan to bring a rose next week," volunteers Wayne, "but don't know how I can sneak it in here without Olive seeing it. Maybe I can drop it off during the day and put it in the fridge."

"I'll take care of the rose," assures Ted. "I have plenty in my back garden."

On the last line this time, Wayne approaches the statue of Our Lady of Recapitulation and with a genuflect full of adoration, he offers his gift to the virgin of repeated sorrows.

The chorus disbands anticipating the arrival of Olive.

Scene: *lights up, church basement, one week later.*

Barbershop chorus in attendance. No Wayne and no Olive. Ted proceeds with warm-ups and the singing of a few tags. "Please don't give my daddy no more wine" and "The Old Songs".

Door swings open - enter Wayne, followed closely by the love of his life, Olive, dressed all in black, including her western boots. She is a buxom cowgirl from Williams Lake, grapevining her way across the linoleum. A chair quickly materializes and Olive is planted square in front of the chorus to the approval of a beaming Wayne, who nudges Ted, questioning in mime, if the rose is in the building.

Olive sits politely on her pedestal through an hour of rehearsal before the big moment is finally thrust upon her.

The quartet rises, approaches the throne of the black Queen, and commences to sing. A rose is visible, tucked behind the back of her gallant knight, Sir Wayne.

Quartet: Heart of my heart, I love you!

The poor woman shudders, looks away, tries to find comfort somewhere in the room other than the four pairs of eyes that are lasering her to the chair. She connects with Our Lady in the corner, longing for the song to end or for the Virgin to swoop down off the wall and carry her to Heaven or the other place.

And now Wayne is moving forward, bending as he brings the rose from behind his back.

Quartet: I can forget you never/ From you I ne'er can sever.

She hesitates, then accepts the rose and the tears flow. Wayne takes her in his arms and the quartet oozes into the final phrase.

Quartet: Say you'll be mine forever, I Love You!

Olive rises suddenly, her cowboy hat askew, and runs from the room. Wayne exits.

Fade to black.

On the following Thursday, Wayne's absence is noted by Bud, the secretary, in the members' attendance book. Ted announces that he has received a Thank You card and reads it during the break to an attentive audience.

Dear Ted and barber shoppers,

Thank you for your song last week. I have never been sung to before and was very embarrassed. I apologize for leaving so abruptly without thanking you all. I am glad Wayne is part of such a wonderful group of fellas. I am home now in Williams Lake where I plan to stay. Perhaps I will see you singing on TV some time in the future.

Regards, Olive

The group finishes rehearsal by working on a new song, "You're the flower of my heart"; the Virgin smiles in her alcove.

While the men close off the evening with "Keep the whole world singing", Wayne is cruising the town in his pickup truck, a faded rose dangling from the rear view mirror. He hums to himself.

1987 - GEISHA

IT is late in February, during the Sunday evening meal that Wayne Lacombe regularly takes with Ted, and his wife Jean, upstairs. While the coffee is dripping, the topic of foreign students is introduced. Ted and Jean are considering hosting a foreign student for two weeks in the spring. They are hoping Wayne can help them out with the hosting by showing the visitor around and providing more of an experience than the two of them could do alone. They consider themselves "over the hill" and out of touch with the pulse of the younger community.

Wayne shows little interest in the proposal until Jean mentions that they are requesting a female university student from Japan. He shifts gears immediately and imagines the Far East, land of the exotic geisha, delicate women who are culturally programmed to please their men. He has heard stories of these women trained in the art of lovemaking who dedicate their lives to promoting pleasure in the men who support them. He is already warming up to the idea of co-hosting. Ted and Jean can feed and house her while he shows her the true north strong and free. He is in-between girlfriends at the moment and open to any new titillation that might come his way. Some of the video rentals he has watched feature Asian beauties with no inhibitions, who utilize erotic devices he has never seen before. He has read that Japanese women, unfettered with Christian morality, willingly give themselves to men, western men in particular.

His evenings are filled with fantasy. He purchases incense from a local counterculture boutique and lights a stick after his shower. He tries to acquire a taste for sake, drinking it both heated and chilled. He rents more movies and not just the adult kind. His rental card is filled with Kung Fu, Judo and Karate flicks. He joins a local Tai Chi club and starts walking barefoot around the house. He is in training he reminds himself. In true samurai fashion he must be worthy of the lotus blossom, who will soon be in his keeping.

Akiko arrives in the first week of April. Wayne does not meet her at the airport as suggested by the Dawsons but makes his first encounter in Ted's terraced back garden where Jean has organized a welcome gathering for Akiko.

It is a warm spring day with a gentle breeze that ruffles the Canadian and Japanese flags Ted has hung from the clothesline.

Wayne is casually dressed: shorts, sandals and a red T-shirt he found at the local thrift shop that reads "ganbatte" in Japanese hiragana. He has no idea of the meaning of the strange characters he sports on his chest but wants to make a good first impression. Ted waves Akiko over to meet Wayne, hoping Wayne's arrival will add some energy to this afternoon's events. So far his well-planned introduction to Canada has gone somewhat flat, with Akiko barely responding to the celebration he and Jean have arranged.

Wayne stands bewildered as his Asian dream woman proceeds across the closely cropped lawn towards him. She is not what he has come to meet. She is not what he has observed in the adult videos. She is not what he wants to spend the next two weeks escorting around the countryside.

Working from the ground up, her bean pole legs end in a hipless waist that give rise to a chestless torso that supports a head with the dorkiest glasses he has ever seen.

"Akiko, I would like to introduce you to Wayne, the man who rents my basement suite."

"Ahh, Wayne-san, I amu hoppy meet you."

"Yeah, likewise."

She begins a bow but then quickly shifts to a handshake. She has been reading the handbook sent by the home stay agency. Wayne takes her hand but refuses to look into her eyes. Instead he stares at her chest. Two nipples can barely be discerned behind a pink blouse that reads in English: "I am want you - NOW!"

"How old are you?"

"I amu twenty-seben yeas orud."

"No shit! I mean really? That's hard to believe. You're about the size my daughter was at age eleven," this time staring at her waist.

"What's your waist size? Never mind. I was expecting someone a little larger, a little fuller. A little more..."

Here Wayne stops and realizes he cannot change the shape of this girl, but he can change his role in Ted and Jean's plans. He can graciously bow out of the arrangement. Make some excuse about working out of town. Perhaps there is a night course he can sign up for.

"Akiko...welcome to Canada. I must talk with Ted for a minute."

He pulls Ted aside and whispers, "I don't think I can do this Ted. She's not really what I expected. I mean she's just a kid."

"Wayne, Akiko is not a kid. She is a graduate from Kansai Women's University. First in her class. She has come to Canada to improve her English so that she can pursue postgraduate work here in B.C. She is one smart woman and we need your help in making sure she has a warm introduction to Canada. So wipe the disappointment off your face and show her around the yard while I get you a beer. We're counting on you, Wayne."

"I don't think so, Ted. I've got somewhere else I need to be."

He escapes to his basement suite in spite of Ted's insistent gestures. Ted leads Akiko back to the small gathering around the barbecue, pointing out his early daffodils and hyacinths.

In his front room Wayne gathers up his latest video rentals, *Wild Women of the Water Trade* and *Tokyo Tiger* and sets off to return them. He stares at the slip covers, erotic displays of willing flesh escaping from colourful kimono. Red pouting lips and dark sensuous eyes stare back at him. He wonders what went wrong?

Wayne's life is a litany of failed visions, disappointments and reversals. He is continually deceived in all his relationships. What appears to be, in fact, never is. What he most desires somehow takes a U-turn and disappears around the next corner. So once again he withdraws, defeated by fate's small joke. He climbs into his truck, throws it into reverse and backs out into the street. From the back yard, a white face surrounded in dark hair follows his retreat.

Later in the evening, Wayne's reverie in front of the television is disturbed by a small knock at the door. He looks through the glass and sees nothing. A further knock and he moves to open the door. Standing before him, the small creature bows, extending her delicate hands that clutch a small rectangular box.

"Wayne-san, a small gift for you from Japan."

"Ah, Akiko."

He fumbles for some appropriate response. She looks a little different from this afternoon. Gone are the glasses and the bizarre T-shirt, replaced by dark jeans and a simple white top. He realizes his hasty departure in the afternoon constitutes a major rudeness in the Japanese code of politeness. Hoping to recover some face he invites her inside.

"Please come in. I was just watching the baseball game."

Akiko removes her shoes, turns them to face the door and surveys the room. Discarded clothing drips from most of the furniture like a nylon moss. Remnants of take-out food populate the flat surfaces. The floor crunches under her footsteps, her socks gathering pockets of sand and dirt that have escaped the cleats of Wayne's work boots.

"Excuse the mess. I haven't gotten around to straightening up this week. I've been busy."

"Daijobu, Wayne-san. It's okay, neh. Please...presento. I hope we can be friends."

Wayne takes the box from Akiko's slender fingers - probably a piano player - he surmises and falls back into the sofa. He examines the box that is wrapped in exquisite gold and orange paper and tied with a purple-knotted cord. He removes the cord and paper which reveals a cloth box, the colour of young ferns. He raises the top of the box and is confronted with thin layers of rice paper beneath which lies a small wooden doll.

Akiko, whose head has been bowed, raises her eyes to watch as Wayne slowly lifts the doll from the box. He seems fascinated by the elegantly carved figure. He strokes the polished surface of the kimono - brilliant red embossed with pale pink cherry blossoms. The face is blank, non-committal, revealing nothing, yet speaking volumes. The figure holds a small open fan as if gesturing to the observer to come closer.

Wayne clutches the Orient within his hands. He smells the wood and is transported to cobble stone streets crowded with tile-roofed houses. Wooden bridges arch over small rocked canals; the cherry trees are in full blossom. All those movies set in the exotic streets of Kyoto come swimming into his senses. Adorned geisha, sliding along the wet stoned alleys in high plat-formed shoes, destined for some dimly lit teahouse overlooking a pond. He is there sitting cross-legged at a low table sipping warm sake from a bamboo cup poured by an Asian beauty.

He looks up into the eyes of the disappointment that sits across from him.

"Akiko, this is very beautiful. Thank you so much."

She bows again, her dark hair slipping across her face. She straightens up and prepares to leave.

"Wayne-san. You would like I make tea for you some time?"

"Yeah, okay. Can I get you a beer or something before you go?"

"Keiko desu. Thank you, no. I must prepare for my first Engurlsh resson tomorrow afternoon. Good night, Wayne-san."

"Good night and thanks for the doll. She's a beaut."

He returns to the doll as Akiko slides into her shoes and departs without a sound.

The next morning Wayne is alarmed by water dripping from his ceiling. He is sitting on the toilet with a magazine when he first notices the moisture beading above his head. Then a few drips and finally a thin stream. When a chunk of gyp rock drops at his feet he is off the seat and out the back door pounding on Ted's screened porch. No answer. Ted is golfing and Jean is arranging flowers at the church.

Wayne opens the screen door, crosses to the back door and enters the kitchen. He can hear the water in the bathroom running at full tilt. He imagines the worst, a burst pipe in the wall or an overflowing toilet - both indicating major damage. He throws open the bathroom door to discover Akiko standing naked in the shower, water spraying everywhere.

"Turn off the water right now!"

He barks out this order and quickly closes the door not wanting to embarrass her further. He continues to shout from behind the closed door.

"Turn off the water! Accident! Water in the basement! I am wet downstairs!"

He struggles to simplify the warning.

"Big Problem! Water in the House! Flood!"

Not sure if he is communicating, he slowly opens the door. The shower has been turned off and Akiko is wrapped in a towel that barely covers her thin porcelain body.

"I'm sorry, Akiko. Water is coming downstairs. You must use the shower curtain. Like this!"

Wayne crosses to the wall, releases the curtain from a hook and slides it across the front of the bathtub. Akiko says nothing; her face reveals nothing. She stands in simple elegance, draped in a white towel, hair piled on top of her head. Not moving.

Wayne retreats to calculate the damage downstairs. He is dumbfounded that someone could be so stupid.

Later when he and Ted attempt further cleanup and repairs, Wayne questions the intelligence of Ted's foreign student. Ted tries to explain what happened.

"In Japan, apparently, the showers are in a room by themselves. There are no curtains or dividers. The water splashes everywhere - off the ceiling, the walls and eventually flows into a drain in the floor. Not a bad system actually. But doesn't quite work in a room with flimsy gyp rock walls."

Several days slip by without a face to face with Akiko and Wayne figures his avoidance strategy is working. He leaves early for work in the morning and remains at the bar until late, ordering food off the menu that he can't afford. He figures this is better than acting as a chaperone to an Asian teenager.

And then the invitation to dinner upstairs. Akiko is preparing Japanese food. It would be nice if he would come.

As Wayne changes into a clean T-shirt he eyeballs the doll figure on his dresser. It's out of place between a second place trophy for a raft race he entered twenty years ago and a plastic 32 Ford Roadster. He picks it up, smells it, then fondles the folds in the kimono.

A gift so appropriate. Given with such grace. Wayne recalls those slender fingers reaching out to him, delicately balancing the carefully wrapped parcel.

He flashes back to Akiko standing naked in the shower. Arms tilted, hands lost in the long dark hair in the act of rinsing shampoo. Like a dancer poised in the moment, awaiting the resumption of the music. Soapy foam runs between her small breasts and down her flat stomach.

There is a thump on the floor above him. Ted is announcing that dinner is almost ready.

Everyone is seated but Akiko who shuffles back and forth to the kitchen in slipper sandals. She wears a bamboo printed housecoat that Jean informs him is a *ukata*, a summer kimono.

Her hair is up with chopsticks jammed through a knot in the back.

She bows to Wayne who kicks his shoes off at the door and takes a seat at the head of the table.

"Itadakimasu."

The first course is a thin soup with chunks of what looks like white cheese floating on the surface.

"Miso soup with tofu and...tama negi."

"Onions," translates Jean.

It looks disgusting to Wayne but he forges ahead, quite enjoying the unfamiliar taste. He requests a second bowl.

Followed by a salad of sorts. Strange textures of bark and wood shavings. A little carrot is recognizable, a mushroom coloured melange woven together with clear stringy noodles. A tangy sauce.

Thankfully the salads are small. Five bites and he's past this hurdle. He smiles at Akiko who has yet to sit down. He nods curtly as he passes her his empty salad bowl.

"Arigado, Akiko-san."

He remembers some simple salutations from tai chi class. She beams at him.

"Do itashimashite, Wayne-san."

The main dish appears.

"Sushi," announces Ted, "and I helped to roll them!"

Plates stacked with cross sections of rice logs appear from the fridge, multi-coloured growth rings of unrecognizable substance are held in place by a thin dark layer of green seaweed.

"We took Akiko down to the docks and bought fish right off the boat. She served raw tuna last night."

"Sashimi," corrects Jean who looks to Akiko for verification.

"Do you have any chicken nuggets?"

Ted smiles sideways and Wayne quickly buttons his lip when he realizes the rudeness of his comment. It is obvious that Akiko has gone to great trouble to prepare this food. She serves Wayne with one each of the delicate rolls and a small helping of pink ginger flakes and a drop of lime green wasabi. She fills his side saucer with soy sauce.

"Mixu, Wayne-san," and she proceeds to demonstrate on her own plate.

Wayne adds a little wasabi to his soy sauce, stirs it around with his chopsticks and dips his sushi into the mix. He bites with conviction and swallows, only to be rewarded with an intense burning that rages up his nostrils.

Ted pours him a beer which he quickly downs.

"Abunai, Wayne-san - be careful - sukoshi dake. A little bit only."

For dessert, green tea and chocolate filled buns. Finally, Wayne launches into something familiar but only to be confronted with another mystery. What he assumed was chocolate turns out to be something much different. Right colour but wrong taste and texture.

"Nato," explains Akiko.

"Bean paste," translates Jean.

Wayne manages to overpower the bun but not without the help of several cups of tea.

"And now Wayne, we would like you to take Akiko somewhere nice. Jean and I will clean up while you young people go out and have a good time."

Ted slips him two twenty dollar bills under the table. Wayne struggles to find an excuse but before he can manufacture one, Akiko has reappeared in jeans and sweatshirt ready to go.

"Iki masho ka? Let's go."

Wayne has been trapped. A victim of international intrigue. This has been Ted's agenda all along. Feed the boy then drop the bomb. Watch him squirm.

Once in the truck, Akiko is the first to speak.

"Wayne-san. I am hoppy to get out of house. Jean and Ted nice people but I am wanting to see za town."

Wayne is uncomfortable but has little room for maneuvers. He quickly runs through the list of locations he can take her without being seen by anyone. The movies - arrive late, leave early. A drive up the mountain. Park above the town and watch a meteor shower. No, she might get the wrong idea...rent a video and go back to his place. That might be safest.

"You like videos, Akiko?"

"Not tonight, Wayne-san. I want to party. Where the action is? Where you go with friends."

"Well, I usually hang out at Tina's Bar. Have a few beers. Listen to the band. Dance a little."

"Okay. Me too!"

This is the last place Wayne wants to take Akiko. His ego would be damaged irreparably. He fears the assumptions that would be made. She looks up at him, her doll like eyes filled with pleading.

"Purease, Wayne-san. I want to see all Canada, not just my home stay house."

He sympathizes with her. He can't imagine being in continual company with Ted and Jean. He wouldn't wish that on anyone. He quickly designs a cover story for his friends.

"This is Akiko. She is staying with my landlord, upstairs. They had an important meeting tonight so asked me to keep an eye on Akiko. I owe them one."

"So you're like...babysitting?"

Lots of laughter around the two tables that have been slid together to make room for Wayne and Akiko. Wayne ignores the baiting and tries to order some beer from Roxanne who is clearing glasses from the table beside him. He hasn't talked to her since their sweaty encounter in the back room of the bar during the Super Bowl party.

And it seems she has no desire to talk with him - ever. She wanders away oblivious to his raised arm and rising voice.

Harrison comes over and takes his order but not before asking Akiko for some ID. She removes her driver's license from her designer bag.

"What the hell is this?"

"Dhis is my duribing ricense."

"Sure it is honey - for all I know it could be your library card. Where's your birth date on here?"

"Right dere. 6 - 11 - 33."

"I don't think so - 1933 - that makes you fifty-two years old. And I'm looking at somebody who doesn't look a day over fourteen."

"No! 33 is year of Emperor: Showa 33. This year, Showa 60. I am twenty seben yeahs orud."

Wayne feels compelled to say something but does not want to become involved. This could be their ticket for leaving. He allows Harrison to do his job.

Akiko is troubled by this scene. She does not like confrontation and has spent most of this ordeal staring into her lap afraid to meet the eyes of the large pot bellied man standing before her. She cannot believe that having a drink in Canada can be so difficult. In Japan she can stop at a drink machine anywhere in the city and purchase as much beer as she wishes without interrogation.

"Wait - I have my correge ID card in my bag. It has western dates written on it, maybe."

Harrison studies the student card under the light at the bar and consults with Tina who gives him the nod. Four bottles of Kokanee appear and two glasses. Akiko rises, grabs a bottle and slowly pours Wayne's glass half full.

"Dozo, Wayne-san. Sank you for bringing me to zizs bar."

With the beer remaining in the bottle she pours her own and raises her glass to Wayne.

"Kampai!"

By now the entire table is engrossed by the proceedings taking place between Akiko and Wayne. Aware of their attention, Akiko raises her glass to the others.

"Kampai!"

The remainder of the table, including Wayne, respond with a loud "Kampai!" Lots of laughter and further raising of the glass each time a sip is taken. The group is enjoying this novelty and Wayne, for the moment, drops his desire to make a quick exit.

Akiko removes her heavy coat to reveal more bizarre English. "Sports Violent! All the day long". Wayne leans forward to be sure he has read correctly.

"Heh, Akiko. What's with the T-shirt?"

"T-shirt bery popular in Japan. Young people want to be more Engurish. Buy clothses with Engurish writing. You rike?"

"Well, it's not my style. Do you know what it means?"

"Japanese rubu sports. Active rife is good rife."

"Whatever you say."

It's nine o'clock and a local band is setting up. Wayne is relieved; he has no idea how to make small talk with this foreign woman. The band cranks up some tunes and several couples start to shuffle around the dance floor. The music is a little too country and western for Wayne's liking but he beats out the rhythm on the table with his left hand, nevertheless.

"Wayne-san, rike to dansu?"

Wayne surveys the crowd. Dancing with Akiko might give his friends the wrong idea.

"Ahhh...No thanks. I injured my leg at work today so I'll just sit."

But before he finishes his sentence a stranger from across the room is already leading Akiko to the dance floor. He drapes himself over her petite frame as she snuggles into his chest. Soon he is lifting her off the ground when he turns. She smiles with the attention and physical excitement. Now he is lifting her light body into the air and swinging her legs around his waist like some rag doll. He is revelling in his power and domination over her malleable torso.

Wayne is overwhelmed with mixed feelings. Should he be rescuing Akiko from this brute? Should he smile along with the others? He sits motionless.

The bulky stranger leans into Akiko in an attempt to kiss her but she turns her head as he buries his lips into her slender neck. She struggles to release herself from his firm grip but he is determined to taste this delicate flower that rests in his grasp. He plunges forward again, this time grabbing her buttocks and pulling her body tighter into his crotch.

Wayne is out of his seat and across the room.

"Hey! Back off man! Give the lady some room. Show a little respect to our visitor, will you!"

"What's it to you, dick head? I'm showing her a real good time here and she's lovin' every minute of it."

Akiko has managed to break loose and Wayne grabs her hand.

"Sorry to disappoint you, asshole, but she's with me! Come on Akiko, it's time to leave."

The brute struggles to save face as a crowd has gathered around the confrontation. Wayne has no desire to prolong this scene and pulls Akiko towards their coats.

"Okay, lover boy - take your chink girlfriend and have a real nice time. Now that I've got her all warmed up for you. She's ready for the full meal."

By the time he is finished, Wayne and Akiko are outside in the parking lot beside the truck.

"Are you all right, Akiko?"

She is silent, staring at him, eyes beginning to fill with tears. He pulls the coat around her "Sports Violent" and lifts her into the passenger seat.

At home Akiko stands on the stairs leading to Ted and Jean's back porch while Wayne locks up the truck. He approaches and stands in front of her on the driveway pavement. They are the same height.

"I am sorry Wayne-san. I make problem. Sank you helpingu me."

She leans forward and kisses him gently on the lips, turns and runs up the steps.

Inside his room, Wayne lifts the doll from the dresser and smiles. He lays it beside him on the pillow and sleeps.

Week two slips by without incident. Wayne watches for Akiko but she has been kept busy by the home stay agency touring the region. Her evenings have been filled with farewell dinners and parties. Friday, after work, Wayne finds a pale mauve envelope on his doorstep.

A miniature folded crane is glued to the flap. Wayne carefully removes the origami creation and opens the envelope. Inside lies an invitation beautifully inscribed with brush and ink.

Wayne-san
Please come to Tea Ceremony
in the garden.
Sunday: 2:00 pm
Akiko

Ted's garden is a terraced affair with rock steps to carry the flower enthusiast from one level to another. On the top layer beneath a full blossomed cherry tree, a large mat has been laid out. On the mat a low table displays an arrangement of lacquered boxes, clay bowls and elegant utensils. A small burner beside the table heats a black kettle. Wayne learns later that Akiko has brought some of this with her from Japan; the rest has been borrowed.

Jean and Ted are already kneeling on the mat and Wayne joins them. Nothing is spoken. There is a stillness in the yard. A small breeze ruffles the cherry blossoms and a few stray petals drift across the mat. Even the yappy dog next door is silent.

Akiko approaches from the top of the garden. She is resplendent in a pink kimono, patterned with white blossoms. A dark red obi is cinched about her waist, a fan tucked into its folds. Her hair is piled above her head and held in place with shiny black combs.

She bows to the altar of tea and to the three guests. Wayne, Ted and Jean respond in turn.

The ceremony begins. Akiko's every movement is a study in refinement. From the raising and turning of the bowls to the folding of the wiping cloth, a simple choreography is maintained as the ritual continues. The grass-like shavings of tea are gently scooped with the narrow bamboo spoon, which is leaned precisely against a lacquered box when finished. Water is added to the leaves and methodically stirred with a whisk until the tea has become a green froth. The bowl is raised and turned and handed to Ted who drinks, reverses the turn and gives the bowl back to Akiko. The bowl is rinsed, wiped and the process is repeated.

Wayne is mesmerized by the repetition of graceful motion. He is pulled into a simple rhythm of lifting, lowering and reaching and soon the world around him begins to disappear. Gone are the frustrations of work, the failures of relationship and even the pain of his own battered ego. All that remains is the colour of silk, lacquer and petals. A peace descends and Wayne is lost in the moment.

When his turn arrives he is unprepared for the bitter salt taste that meets his lips and passes over his gums. He was expecting something else. Much like the recurring patterns in his own life, he muses. He has always been expecting something else.

The harshness of the tea is followed by a sweet cake that melts in his mouth and removes the bitterness of the drink. He sits back on his heels and surveys the yard. The breeze has picked up and the pink petals are dropping more frequently. They stick to Akiko's hair and drop in the bowl that she wipes clean. The ritual of restoration is complete, every item returned to its starting position. Akiko rises and kneels before Wayne.

"You like tea ceremony, Wayne-san?"

"Very much Akiko. You were beautiful...you are beautiful, and I am so glad to meet you."

Everyone has returned to the starting position, thinks Ted. The sun is shining; a small breeze is blowing. Wayne and Akiko meeting in the garden for the first time. Only this time Akiko leaves tomorrow.

The farewell is short and simple. Akiko presents Wayne with the fan that is folded in her obi. Wayne removes a petal from her hair and kisses her on the cheek.

"Arigato, Akiko-san. Arigato."

"Ganbatte, Wayne-san. Do your best."

1988 - ANGEL

WAYNE Lacombe lies stiff on a hospital bed staring at a white ceiling. The ceiling tiles form the grid and anchor of his altered existence, the rigid rectangles shaping his new world view. Snowflake perforations blink from the white dome under which he lies, watching him shift gently when the pain momentarily subsides.

Wayne has been here for six days now and although he can turn his head to take in the remainder of the room, he always returns to the white tiles, hoping to find in their void the reason for his crippling condition.

Embedded in the ceiling, like an aluminum petalled daisy, one sprinkler head peers down upon his checkered blankets and blue hospital gown. For most of the day he is alone with the sprinkler head and his own imaginings. At these times he floats in a white world with white trees and white clouds. A white face in a white hood and a white scarf peers down on his body and speaks in a frozen language. He recognizes nothing.

Sometimes, the dull peach dividing curtain slides along its track whenever he or his room mate, Karl, require personal space - to relieve themselves, to undergo bladder scans, or engage in more intimate rendezvous with a bed pan.

Any new arrival in the room is a grand excitement. A new face, even a cart bearing the latest in technical equipment is a welcome intrusion. But for Wayne, he waits with anticipation for the arrival of the next shift of nurses. Who might swim into his shrunken world? A pretty girl with a thermometer or an aged crone with a suppository? He makes small talk with them all. Anything to hold them in the room a bit longer than necessary, to delay his return to the ceiling tiles.

On day two, Stephanie stepped into his life and he felt he could stay here at St. Clements forever. She was all smiles and good vibes; she radiated care and concern. She responded to his every whim: fed him breakfast, held his toothbrush, took his pulse. He reveled in his evening wash, her gentle hands guiding the warm face cloth over his pain wracked body. Wayne prolonged these baptisms as long as possible. The ceiling tiles dissolved and the heavens opened up to reveal blue skies and endless horizons. At the end of these visions the white face would reappear and speak to him in soft words, sometimes holding his hand and kissing his cheek. And when the face finally vanished he would call out for Stephanie, over and over until the night nurse would give him a sleeping pill.

Stephanie, he learned later, was not the owner of the white face. She was a student in her last year of nursing at the local university. Rehab ward constituted her final practicum. Four days on and four days off. Twelve hour shifts. For three more days she listened to his complaints, laughed at his lame attempts at humor and satisfied his every desire...well, not quite. He hadn't mustered enough resolve to request that she remove her top while massaging his legs after the evening wash ritual.

And then she was gone, replaced today by Muriel the Man Handler who Wayne swears was in construction before taking up nursing. She approaches every task with rolled up sleeves and a fierce expression of purpose. "Get the Job Done" is tattooed on her left bicep and that she does.

Wayne's privates are raw following Muriel's first evening wash. She stands leering as he downs the last drops of the toxic laxative, making him lick out the remains in the paper cup with his tongue. And toothbrush? Forget it. Wayne is forced to roll and fetch from his drawer the tools he needs to "get the job done". Gone are those evenings of banter and innuendo. Instead, Wayne's room has become a combat zone. Muriel and her army of invasive devices pitted against a defenseless Wayne outstretched in his misery. Tied like some pathetic Gulliver, he lies exposed to all means of torture and ridicule.

Wayne longs for another shift change.

The ceiling tiles become a refuge; he is pulled into their vast landscape of nothingness - sheet after sheet of paper toweling provide some comfort to the continuing ordeal that rages around him. Deeper and deeper into the drifts of angel hair he searches for the angel with the white face and some answers to his broken spine.

On day eight Muriel introduces him to the Jewett Brace, a hold over from the Inquisition. The metal framed device is designed to clasp the torso like an iron maiden, securing the perimeter, so to speak, to prevent internal damage to the spinal column. Once ensconced in this shell, Wayne imagines himself a medieval knight in readiness for a joust. But no lance appears and no Stephanie, his Lady of Gentle Strokes. He must do battle accompanied only by her love token, a damp face cloth he keeps under his pillow.

Securing Wayne in his brace is no mean task. Muriel latches the bolt in the left side while her sidekick, Martine, reefs down on the hooks on the right. This final exertion ejects Wayne's tongue from his mouth and makes his hair stand on end. Breathing becomes a challenge. He works for each breath like some diver in an aqua-lung. But the pain has just begun.

"Today, you will rise from the bed and sit on its edge," commands Muriel.

"You gotta be kidding," wheezes Wayne.

"Roll over on your side. Pull yourself to a sitting position," she instructs.

He dutifully rolls over; the sitting, however, requires more stamina. He fights the lightheadedness as he pulls his body from the damp wrinkled sheets. The room swims, Muriel's face oscillating between John Candy and Genghis Khan. Hands on her hips, she is speaking in tongues. Wayne's body approaches the vertical as the pain mounts.

"Now, hold it for five minutes," she proclaims.

The second hand on the decrepit clock on the wall jerks its way around the face. Wayne feels the heat rising in his own face, the shaking barely under control. At three minutes he collapses on his left side, totally exhausted.

"Not good enough," Muriel declares. "Try it again."

Wayne stares at her incredulously until her sidekick takes his arm and starts to lift.

"No! Stop!" blares Muriel. "He must do it on his own."

And so Wayne bites his lip and makes the effort pulling himself eighty degrees from the bed.

"That's it," he musters. "I can go no further."

"Okay, we try again later. Remove the brace. Record his performance. We must have him sitting vertical for the X-rays tomorrow."

The two matrons goose step from the room, clipboards under their arms.

Wayne log rolls into his familiar slot and loses himself in the vast movie screen of ceiling tiles. The film has just begun and the credits are rolling. "A Quick Release Morphine Production". Stacks of vertebrae appear floating in space. Nerves like colour coded telephone wires pulsate between them like car lights on the freeway at night. The voice over begins, Anglo-Indian.

"The lumbar one marks the end of the spinal cord and the beginning of the spinal canal. This is a major transition point and is usually the first victim of any serious fall. (A red circle appears around lumbar one and the camera zooms in.) In your case, lumbar one has not only fractured but also burst. (The close up shows a mushroom cloud rising from lumbar one with fragments of bone chips emerging and drifting away.) There is some concern that some of the chips may be encroaching on the spinal canal."

The screen fades to white leaving a brown face suspended in front of the ceiling tiles.

"Good afternoon, Mr. Lacombe, I am Dr. Swarma, the neurosurgeon here at the hospital. I have just been looking at your X-rays and CAT scan. I would like to know more of what is happening at lumbar one. I have ordered an MRI for you and more X-rays. Can you tell me about how you landed when you fell?"

Wayne's mind is a blur. During moments of consciousness he recalls descending switchbacks in the bed of a truck. The mountain is draped in snow; the flakes obliterate his view of anything prior to his ride to the hospital.

"I am sorry Doctor, I don't remember anything about the fall."

"I will be talking to you soon. Good day, sir."

"Thank you, Doctor."

Wayne spends a fitful night, the rising pressure in his abdomen due to a lack of movement in his bowels, exerts pressure on his bladder, which forces him to pee small amounts every hour. Flushing his bladder involves a series of contortions that eventually result in a small trickle into a plastic bottle with an offset neck.

In Wayne's case he rolls to his left side, extends his left leg while raising his right leg into the air. A gentle nudging of the bottle against his bladder usually generates marginal outflow. Often while suspended in this position, nurses come and go. He soon becomes known as the acrobat and one petite cleaning woman simply calls him "Houdini".

Following each void, the scanning machine appears, ready to measure the remaining fluid in his bladder. This procedure involves applying copious amounts of cold jelly to a plastic roller that is maneuvered over his stomach searching for the center of his bladder. Numbers are registered on a screen - 160 ml.

"Not good enough Mr. Lacombe. We need to get those numbers under one hundred or the catheter will be used."

Wayne tries harder.

Visitors come and go in the backdrop of the ceiling tiles and speak to him in his morphine stupor. Ted, his landlord and wife, Jean, interrupt his journey along the ceiling seams on more than one occasion but he is unaware of who they are.

"Wayne, can you hear me? We've brought you some fruit and Jean has picked some flowers from her garden. How are you, my boy?"

"The place doesn't seem the same without you, Wayne."

Wayne, the son they never had, smiles a brief grin, hoping to discover the white face in their midst.

"Don't worry about your Hydro bill, Wayne. It's all been taken care of. And forget about this month's rent. We'll wait until you are back on your feet."

Wayne floats back to the snowstorm that drifts across his ceiling. If only he could find his way back home - back through the void. He tries to retrace his steps, but his footprints have been covered with snow. If only he could locate the line of memory that would connect him with the event that propelled him into this bed.

The stretcher man arrives early in the morning. Derrick, from transport, spends his days taxiing patients from one department to another. He negotiates the crowded hallways from Rehab to Imaging, avoiding all manner of oncoming traffic. Wayne follows the ceiling tiles along the circuitous route and mouths the signs that dangle from the walls: Laundry, Food Services, Asthma Clinic, Chapel, Transplants, X-ray and finally Magnetic Resonance Imagining.

"Hey there, I'm John, one of the MRI techs. How's it going today? Can you sit up?"

"Ahhhh...No!"

"That will be a log roll, Frank - on 'three'. Cross your arms on your chest Mr. Lacombe. Hold still. Now you'll be about forty minutes in the tube, during which time you must remain perfectly still. Okay? Have you been given an anxiety pill?"

Wayne recalls the small pebble that had been slipped under his tongue before he left his room. Now earplugs are stuffed into his ears.

"Suffer from claustrophobia, Wayne?"

Wayne flashes back to fearful struggles inside a damp mummy bag on wet mornings in the mountains, and caving in narrow tunnels above Twin Lakes. He tries to erase these memories from his mind as the board on which he lies begins its journey deep inside the MRI machine.

He conjures pleasant thoughts, remembering the girls in his life, slowly removing their clothing and following the contours of their bodies. He begins with Tracey.

Inside the tube, blue lights are flashing like some miniature runway. When the hatch is sealed, the resonating begins - subterranean pulsations of African rhythms, followed by counter beats laid over the first series of staccato. Wayne feels a connection with the tune, something both alien and familiar. He recalls the communication sound sequence from the movie *Close Encounters of a Third Kind*. He listens for the pattern to recur. The pace increases then subsides only to begin again an octave higher.

He tries to return to Tracey's distinctive hip line and buttock cleft but is drawn once more into the overpowering pulsations that envelope him. He resists the desire to articulate the rhythm with his dormant fingers.

Soon it is over. His body is removed from the cocoon, log rolled back onto the stretcher and wheeled down the corridor, his eyes retracing the ceiling tiles that lead back to his room.

Stephanie is there to unload him from the stretcher. The yellow rubber sheet slides him back into his bed and the familiar surroundings.

"How are you feeling today, Wayne? Can I get you anything?"

"A beer and a bag of pretzels, please."

"Would you settle for a wild berry juice?"

"Sure. When did you come on shift?"

"This morning at 7:00. But I'm working the ward across the hall. Just thought I would check in on you."

"Thanks, Steph. I guess you won't be doing my scanning today or my bathing?"

"I'm afraid not, Wayne. Your physiotherapist will be in this morning with a plan for your rehab. I think that includes washing yourself."

"Really? How am I supposed to do that? I can barely sit up."

"Work with her Wayne. You'll be surprised at what you can accomplish."

By late afternoon Wayne is upright, shuffling the hallways behind a four wheeled walker. He is accompanied by Miss July, a physiotherapist from the cover of Penthouse Magazine whose encouragement has lifted him miraculously from the bed and propelled him out the door of his room.

"Slow down Wayne. This is not a race," Miss July cautions.

Wayne complies, looking across at his new companion strutting down the runway beside him. He imagines this tall brunette modeling seasonal body braces for *Rehab Monthly*. Lost in the grace of her stride, he sends his walker crashing into a portable IV stand, thankfully unoccupied at the time.

"Wayne, stay in control. One step at a time. Breathe easy."

"But Miss July, I can't take my eyes off of you and this damn Jewett brace won't allow me to take anything but shallow pants."

"Its purpose is to keep you erect in a posture of extension."

Wayne has been erect ever since Miss July dressed him in his brace and raised him from the dead.

The walk is short. He surveys his surroundings from a vertical position for the first time: the lobby, television, nurses' station, and other patients in various stages of recovery. Most push walkers, some propel themselves in wheel chairs while others are pushed, their rigid bodies strapped from ankle to forehead. One young man dribbles as he is wheeled towards the walk-in bath.

Miss July is full of praise as Wayne follows her trim derriere back to his room. He collapses on the bed retaining his perfect body alignment.

"Let's keep the brace on for a few more hours," says Miss July. "I want you to take another little walk after dinner."

"When will I see you again, Miss July?"

"Tomorrow morning at 9:30 sharp. Meet me in the Physio gym after breakfast. Nurse Muriel will strap you in and bring you a basin of water. I expect you to be clean, dressed and fed before our appointment, and Wayne, my name is Julie not July."

She vanishes like a mirage on the desert of white ceiling tiles and Wayne finds himself lost once again, making his way across the landscape, pushing into the past, looking for answers.

He is winding his way up a hill in his old Ford pick up. He is alone, a coffee mug wedged in his crotch. There is snow on the road and he has had to stop and put the truck into four-wheel drive. He is climbing to the trail head where an old log cabin acts as a shelter and storage shed for the small guiding company with which he contracts summer work.

He is alone but senses that he is not alone. Someone sits in the passenger seat. He cannot see the face. A hood and scarf make identification impossible. The radio plays "Country road, Take me home". Wayne sings along, faking the words when he is lost, "West Virginia, mountain llama". His passenger appears to laugh but he cannot place the voice.

The cabin rises before him and he remembers why he has made this difficult run up the mountain so late in the season. The roof is leaking. He's been hired to tarp it down before the heavy snows descend. The roof already has several inches of snow on it and he realizes that it will have to be removed before the tarps go on, not an easy feat on a metal roof.

The ladder is tossed from the truck box. Wayne unlocks the cabin and locates the old broom in the corner by the wood stove. This will have to do. As he begins the slow climb up the ladder and on to the peak the screen fades and Wayne falls into a sleep.

"Hey! Houdini, it's dinner time. They aren't serving you in the room any more. You have to eat in the dining hall."

Wayne shuffles down the hallway to join his crippled colleagues. He finds a vacant place beside an older patient, similarly caged in a Jewett Brace.

"Hello," a Russian accent. "You must be new. My name is Peter."

"Ahhh...I've been here for over a week. This is my first day out of my bed."

"Oh really! You are doing very well. Last week I am tripping in the elevator. The machine is stopped eighteen inches from floor and I step out and fall. I am a mess. I live in condo with my wife. She has walker, now she fall. I am not there to help. They won't let me go home."

"I'm sorry. Is there someone who can look in on her?"

"Neighbour is never home. We used to have farm. Neighbour live far away but always stop by to chat and coffee. Now neighbour on other side of wall and we never see."

"Yes, that is strange. Why did you move from the farm?"

"Everyone say we are too old to live alone on the farm. We are more alone now, wish we were back on the farm. I still call the farm my home."

"I understand."

"Listen, young man. I advice to you. Don't ever sell your land. Once it is gone, it is gone. Make yourself a home and hang on to it."

Peter is interrupted by Nurse Muriel. She is distributing pills from a rolling cabinet. The cabinet is locked; the keys jingle from Nurse Muriel's wrist. Wayne surveys the room, observing the myriad of capsules being consumed at this one meal.

"Mr. Lacombe. So good to see you up and getting the job done. I have the special for you tonight. One slow release morphine, one quick release morphine, two red stool softeners, and a shot of high-test laxative, maple flavoured."

"Why thank you, Brunhilde. I look forward to our arm wrestling tournament tomorrow morning."

Peter moves off for his blood pressure check, while Wayne downs his evening cocktail. A wheel chair rolls up beside him as he winces from the last drops of laxative.

"Hey, mister, can you drive me back to the bar?"

"Pardon?"

"I need a lift back to the bar."

The wheel chair occupant is the young man who dribbles. He stares past Wayne's left shoulder.

"I am unable to drive right now. I have a broken back."

"But you drove us here. I need to get back to the bar. It's the only way I can find my way home."

"I'm sorry. I can't drive. I think we should just stay here a bit longer."

Stephanie approaches and grips the wheel chair by the handles. "OK, Michael, let's go and get you cleaned up for bed, shall we?" She addresses Wayne as she turns away. "Motorcycle accident."

Wayne is left alone at the table. The patients have drifted off to mysterious rooms that open onto the main corridor. His short walk takes him down the hall towards Physio then out the north wing to Prosthetics and finally back to his room where Martine removes his brace, refills his water cup and empties his plastic urinal.

"I'll be back later with a sleeping pill. Here is your toothbrush and toothpaste. Good luck."

He tries to read a *Sports Illustrated* magazine he found in the lobby. A special ski supplement sucks him into a snow bank where he lies until Martine returns with a sleeping pill. She pulls the light chain and he is back on the roof pushing the broom down the steep pitch, trying to jettison the snow off the eaves.

And now he is slipping, sliding down the metal, his foot catching the ladder that redirects his fall towards the woodpile and onto a snow covered stump used for splitting kindling.

He lies in the snow, unable to move, the pain overwhelming his attempts to remain conscious. He knows he is alone, but as his vision fades he sees a hooded face looking into his own.

"Wayne," it says. "I will go for help."

"Angel, Angel," Wayne manages to utter before the snow encompasses everything and he is lost.

He is now shouting "Angel" at the top of his lungs while squirming in his bed and flailing at the ceiling tiles. The nursing response is immediate; two nurses are holding him down while another nurse prepares an injection.

The intercom sounds the alarm. "Code White, Code White in Rehab, Code White."

Wayne falls back on his bed and sleeps.

He awakes to find Dr. Swarma and Muriel standing over him talking without volume.

"Mr. Lacombe, I am wanting to know what happened last night," queries the doctor.

"Yes, Mr. Wayne. Please explain your behavior and why I have two nurses with bruises this morning."

"I remember, I remember what happened. I fell from the roof. Fell on the woodpile. And Angel saved me...my white angel. She went for help and they came to rescue me."

"Who is Angel? You were brought here by some snowmobilers who happened to be checking out the snow base on the trails the day you fell."

"I don't know who she is but she was there. She spoke to me. She must have been in my truck when we drove up the hill. I had just forgotten."

"There was no one around when you were found, Wayne. You were barely conscious, lying in the snow. You are a lucky man that they came along when they did. They rolled you onto a plank, slid you into the bed of their truck and drove you to the hospital."

"That's not true. She was there. I can still see her in the ceiling tiles. She has been here to visit me. I know what I am talking about."

And now Dr. Swarma is conversing with the Man Handler at the foot of the bed. They break, the doctor returning to his side.

"Mr. Lacombe. The MRI shows some major pinching of the spinal canal but not enough to warrant surgery. You are indeed fortunate. I will have the nurse decrease your morphine intake and perhaps we can think about releasing you in a few days after Physio has you moving without the walker. You must remain in the brace at all times other than sleeping. We will reassess your fracture in three months time. By this time next year you will be as right as rain. Good day, sir."

Muriel grabs the Jewett from the shelf and turns to face him, arms bulging with purpose.

"And now trouble maker, let's strap you into this brace and get you to breakfast. Maybe Angel will join you this morning. Perhaps she can hold your hand while she spoon-feeds you your cream of wheat."

Muriel exits Wayne's room.

"Just call me Angel of the morning, Angel," trailing from her lips as she moves down the hall.

1989 - IT'S NOT OVER UNTIL...

ERIN Lacombe is struggling with math. Math 12. Erin's problem soon became the problem of her father, Wayne Lacombe, when she moved in with him three months ago. She had left her mother's house in the Interior because she was tired of being "ragged on", she told Wayne late on the night of her arrival in early March. Wayne's time with his daughter has been limited since his wife left him eight years ago - the alternate Christmases, a week every summer and the odd spring break. Now she is a permanent resident in the basement suite along with her spineless father. He has given up his bedroom and sleeps on the couch in front of the TV, which is where he spent most of his time anyway while recovering from his back injury. At least he can walk, drive and run errands for his outfitting employer.

Erin was called in to see Mr. Watkins, her math teacher, last week after the second failing progress report that had been sent home received no response.

Allan Watkins is a good teacher, organized and supportive. He takes every effort to make his students accountable for their performance or lack thereof. He wants his charges to be successful and goes out of his way to be available before and after school as well as at noon hour to provide extra help for students like Erin.

She sits before him, an innocent calm radiating from her heavily made up face. She has taken over Wayne's bathroom at the basement suite and stocked it with her contribution to sustaining the cosmetic industry - every conceivable eye, skin, lip and hair product. She dresses for every occasion and high school is one long fashion runway.

"Did your parents receive the last progress report, Erin?" begins Mr. Watkins.

Erin leans forward and places her cheeks in her hands exposing the round spheres of her ample breasts.

"I don't know," she whispers.

"Erin, I'm going to have to ask you to do up the top two buttons of your blouse if you are going to sit like that."

Allan is no prude but is taking full precaution against any student reprisal. Recently, several girls have complained to the counselor about male teachers looking down their blouses. A teacher in another district has had to answer to charges laid by the College of Teachers.

Erin sits up and slowly buttons up.

"This is serious, Erin. There are only four weeks left in the semester and you are failing this course. There has been no improvement in your performance since coming to this school in March. I have encouraged you to come and see me after school or in the morning and you have yet to make an appearance. My progress reports home have had no effect."

Silence. Allan Watkins builds to a dramatic climax. He rises from his chair and sits on the corner of his desk.

"If you do not pass math this semester, you will not graduate," he declares.

And then the tears burst forth, carrying eye shadow, mascara, blush and lip gloss down the cheeks and into the corners of the mouth and onto the desk top.

"I have to graduate, Mr. Watkins. I just have to. If I don't, my mother will never let me forget it. She said I would fail here. And then my father will send me back to Cranbrook."

"You live with your father now, do you?" queries Mr. Watkins.

"Yes. It's OK, I guess," she responds between sniffs, "but he can't help me. He can't do this math any better than me. I just don't get it. It's too hard and I have too much to catch up. I'm not going to graduate. I'm just a loser." More tears.

"Now, let's not lose hope, Erin," says Mr. Watkins, reaching for the box of tissue he keeps on his desk for runny noses during test periods.

"Perhaps I should talk with your father. He could arrange for a tutor who along with extra help from me might be enough to earn you a passing grade before the provincial exam in June."

Allan is not sure about the sincerity of these tears. His long experience has taught him that female tears are one of the chief sympathy tactics utilized by the gentler sex to soften a teacher's will. Nevertheless, he calls Wayne, hoping to elicit a conference with he and Erin. Failing that, a promise to secure a tutor immediately. Wayne is non-committal regarding a conference, claiming that he works out of town with no set schedule. He halfheartedly says that he will search out a tutor for Erin.

It's Ted who suggests the name of a tutor he knows from church, adding that he will pay the necessary costs to get Erin back on track in math. Wayne is appreciative and mumbles something about making it up doing yard work.

Gwen Sawchuck is a fully certified teacher who just can't seem to crack the TOC list, let alone secure a permanent position in the school district. She lives at home with her aging parents, tutoring when the opportunity arises. She is a pretty, unhappy woman, owing in part to her inability to launch her career and also to the fact that she is considerably overweight. As an only child she has been saddled with the care and maintenance of her elderly parents. She still lives at home which allows for little social life and no real friends. Although she is only thirty-four, permanent frown wrinkles have etched themselves into her attractive face.

She takes the job as Erin's tutor, without questions, even though her degree is in English and agrees to meet her Tuesday evening at the basement suite. Twenty dollars an hour she tells Erin.

She arrives, shortly before 7:00 pm to find Erin and Wayne eating from a pizza box and sucking on cans of Coke. Wayne moves to open the door in order to check her out, anticipating a possible conquest. He still fancies himself a ladies' man. He is immediately hopeful when he sees her face through the door window, but is quickly deflated when the open door reveals the girth of her attached body. His vision of romancing the schoolteacher retreats to the kitchen where he busies himself with the breakfast dishes while Erin offers Gwen some pizza.

"No thank you," declines Gwen, "I think we should get right to work, don't you? Is that your father?"

"Yes. Dad, this is Gwen. She'll be my tutor for the next month. My Dad, Wayne."

"Hi Gwen," slurs Wayne, brushing pizza from his lower lip with a dishrag. "Good luck!"

"Pleased to meet you, Mr. Lacombe. Perhaps you would like to sit in on our session so that you can help Erin between our meetings!"

"Gee, I don't think I can do that," admits Wayne.

He is planning on an evening at the pool, soaking in the hot tub, lounging in the steam room and hustling the unmarried lifeguards – all part of his personal rehab.

"Come on Dad, you owe me, big time. Mom would do this for me," taunts Erin.

The continuing guilt trip. Erin has learned some lessons well. Playing one parent off against the other has assured her of many victories.

So Wayne reluctantly becomes a student once again, balancing "a" squared with "b" squared and juggling "x" to all its powers.

Gwen reviews the homework with Erin and manages to successfully solve some challenging quadratic equations. She has a good memory and pulls operational sequences from her high school math data bank deep in the recesses of her mind. Realizing she needs some further direction, she suggests to Erin that they make an appointment to see Mr. Watkins together in order to review the material that needs to be covered for the exam. They decide two nights a week would be a minimum and maybe more as the exam day draws near.

Wayne catches on quickly and seems to be enjoying himself, sometimes finding the answer before Erin. He is almost having a good time. He even brews some tea for them all and smears jam on the left over pizza crusts.

Before departure, Wayne pulls Gwen into the hallway to discuss payment.

"I'm a little short this week," he confides. "My landlord said he would help out but he's away for a few days. Can I give you a ten tonight and perhaps the rest on Thursday?"

Gwen is reluctant to enter into any deals with this questionable father, but realizes that something is better than nothing. She takes the money and proposes an arrangement.

"I'll tell you what, Mr. Lacombe. If you can come to my house and clean all the outside windows this week, I'll call tonight's lesson square."

Gwen had been dreading the climb to the upstairs windows on the aluminum ladder all spring. The last time she had raised her body to the fifth rung the strain had been too much, warping the frame to the point that the ladder would not retract. She cannot visualize herself on that ladder ever again.

"Well," says Wayne, "I guess that could be arranged. Maybe there are other jobs you need done around the place. I'm pretty handy when I put my mind to it."

He looks around the basement suite and realizes he hasn't been too handy of late. He hasn't been able to put his mind to anything since Erin moved in.

"Sure," says Gwen. "See you Thursday, Erin, and try to make that appointment with Mr. Watkins for Friday after school."

She ambles down the sidewalk and struggles in behind the wheel of her parents' car.

On Thursday, in spite of a recurring fear of heights since his accident, Wayne washes the windows, cleaning the gutters while he's up the ladder and has coffee with Gwen's parents. He promises to return next week to mow the lawns and take their old hot water tank to the dump. Old Mr. Sawchuck waves to him as he pulls out of the driveway.

Thursday night the threesome tackle geometric functions. The house is noticeably tidier. The countertops are cleared and the dishes have all been put away. Wayne has done his homework and has a firm handle on the X and Y axis and actually takes over part of the lesson. While sipping jasmine tea, Wayne asks Gwen if she has any girlfriends who aren't presently married.

On Friday after school, following a hectic day without a break, two parent phone calls and a noon meeting for the bursary committee, Allan Watkins awaits the arrival of Erin and her new tutor. He pulls out the answer key for a worksheet of sample questions from previous provincial exams and starts calculating answers when Erin and Gwen appear at his door. He was hoping they could circle up three desks to look over the curriculum, but assessing the size of Gwen as she enters, he quickly rolls his own chair into place so that she will not have to squeeze herself into a student desk.

The meeting goes well. Gwen catches on fast to what is expected. Erin remains in the background until Allan suggests she try some of the sample questions while he and Gwen are watching and can coach her along.

On the first question, after numerous attempts, Erin goes to pieces. Pink erasure flakes blanket the page as she makes change after change to the number and letter sequences.

83

The pencil breaks. She sobs giant tears onto the Math Fundamentals Textbook.

"I can't do it, I just can't do it!" she protests. "I'm going to fail! I'm not going to graduate!"

She wipes her nose on her sleeve but the tears continue to roll from her cheeks.

Allan fumbles for some reassurance, some positive uplifting advice that will carry everyone through this awkward moment. He digs deep into the realm of clichés, the thesaurus of clever sayings, the grab bag of one-liners and snatches one at random.

"Erin, it's going to be alright. Don't worry. Remember what they say. 'It's not over until the fat lady sings'."

These last words emerge just as he turns to face Gwendolyn Sawchuck. These last words emerge even as he is trying to pull them back into his mouth. These last words emerge into a dreadful void of silent realization and embarrassment. Allan's eyes drop immediately from the woman before him. His fingers fiddle with a pocket calculator on the desk as he struggles to formulate some kind of apology. But none is forthcoming. Gwen sidesteps the comment as if she has not heard it and launches into verbal comfort for Erin.

"It's okay Erin, I used to cry over math, too. In fact, I think everyone cries about math at some time in their schooling. Isn't that right Mr. Watkins? Mr. Watkins?"

"Oh! Yes, yes! Math is the only subject that the majority of students cry about," he concurs. "My own children cry about math. My wife cried about math. I've even thought about crying on several occasions." (And I'd like to cry right now, he would like to say.)

A long pause.

"I am so sorry, Ms. Sawchuck. I'm afraid my comment was totally inappropriate; it just slipped out without thinking," Allan manages with his most sincere tone, the one he saves for parents and senior administrators.

Gwen evades the apology with the same aplomb as before and plunges right into a plan for raising Erin's grade in Math 12. It is agreed that she will re-sit the last two tests and dates are written in Mr. Watkins' daybook. Gwen takes the sheet of sample questions as well as Erin's previous failed tests and rises to leave.

"Thank you Mr. Watkins. You have been most helpful. I'm sure Erin will be ready for the retests and that she *will* pass the provincial exam. Goodbye."

Outside, in the parking lot, they both breathe relief. Erin commiserates with Gwen and invites her back to the basement suite for tea. Gwen smiles, the hurt seeping out the sides of her lips. She is no stranger to fat jokes, although she realizes the Watkins barb was not intentional. She is a large woman but not impervious to pain.

Later, when the tea is drunk, the review sheet complete and the friendship firmly established, Erin suggests some make-up tips. She takes Gwen into the bathroom and they experiment. Gwen's hair is swept off her face, a striking face once out in the open, a face which Erin embellishes with all the skill and tools at her command. A little colour here, a little accent there. Gwen's eyes are miraculously released from the frown that has dominated her life since university. Her lips swell into a succulent tease that brings a shade of embarrassment to her cheeks when she catches a glimpse of herself in the mirror. But all in all she likes what she sees. A makeover has been long overdue. Something new may yet be on the horizon. Erin's knowledge of fashion and cosmetics soon transforms the dowdy tutor into someone that Wayne does not recognize when he returns home from work. Gwen walks right past him and out the door. She walks all the way home. In fact she walks almost everywhere now.

When Erin and Gwen meet, for lessons or just tea, they laugh. The numbers on the homework page fall into a rhythm, marching towards their intended solution. Wayne continues his chores at the Sawchuck home and takes a liking to Gwen's dad. The two of them stop for coffee at Tim Hortons after grocery shopping on Tuesdays. He even stays with the old couple in the evenings while Gwen is cramming with Erin long into the night as the final exam approaches.

Erin passes her provincial exam. Mr. Watkins puts in a favourable word to his superiors, some strings are pulled and a much slimmer Gwen is offered a temporary teaching position for the coming year.

It's even rumoured that Gwen has been seen on occasion sitting in the cab of an '84 Ford pick up with Wayne at the wheel, the two of them singing along to an old "Hits from the 70's" cassette tape.

1990 - ISIS

WAYNE Lacombe's brother, Ken, works in Egypt. He and his wife, Sylvia, have called Cairo their home for the past five years. Ken, a geologist, works in oil exploration and Sylvia has secured a local hire position at an international school in Maadi. Wayne sees them each summer when on home leave. They usually sip a few beers in the backyard of Wayne's basement suite, a beautifully groomed garden of paths and rock terraces meticulously maintained by Ted.

Every summer the topic of Wayne's visit to Egypt comes up in the conversation. Wayne shrugs with a maybe, opening another beer with a twist, not sure how much he should reveal regarding his personal finances. Ken has done well with his life, completed university, married an energetic woman with a career and travelled most of the world. Wayne, the university dropout, has stumbled from one disaster to another.

He dropped out of university to marry his pregnant girlfriend, a relationship that soon soured and he has since struggled to find some stability in his drifting existence. He worked concrete and construction for a time, wheeling tons of grey matter on job sites and realized he had more grey matter than pouring concrete required. A brief stint at the local college earned him a diploma in recreational management and he still spends his summers guiding overweight tourists into the mountains and out to the offshore islands in kayaks. For the rest of the year, however, he has yet to find permanent employment, picking up work here and there. He still has buddies in construction who look out for him, throwing the odd framing job his way.

To say the least, Wayne is in no position to travel, unless it's up a logging road in his pick up truck to fish some backcountry lake. But the offer, nevertheless, is made by Ken each summer, seconded by Sylvia; last year was no different.

"You know we're not going to be there forever, Wayne. One year more, two at tops. Your chances are dwindling."

Doesn't Wayne know it. With the arrival of his teenage daughter last spring, his sporadic income barely covers the expense of a case of beer at the end of the week. His chances have been dwindling ever since his wife walked out ten years ago.

"Gee, Ken. I don't really think I want to see Egypt. The heat must be unbearable; I don't speak the language. Airfares are really high right now."

"Have we got a deal for you, Wayne." Ken nods to his wife. "We have accumulated so many air miles that we want to share them with you. Your flights won't cost you a thing. You can stay at our place and your only expenses will be some weekend travel that will be minimal because we get resident's rates on all accommodation within the country."

"What do you say?" concludes Sylvia. In the fall the weather is magnificent, not too hot and every day is a sunny day."

Wayne twirls his empty beer bottle in his lap, takes a look at the humming bird oscillating in front of the red bird feeder and ponders his life. He's not going anywhere and he hasn't been anywhere. He's spinning his wheels, flapping his wings but remaining stationary. He has just broken up with Georgia, the latest in a long string of relationships that he has abused since his divorce. His eighteen-year-old daughter, Erin, has been more successful than he has. Since graduation in June, she has found permanent work, something he has been unable to do since high school. Besides, she likes her work - doing makeovers at the mall's beauty salon.

Wayne realizes *he* needs a makeover, a turning point, a shot of cortisone to stop the recurring pattern of his endless failure.

He opens another beer.

Why not go to Egypt? After this season of guiding he should have some ready cash. Erin can stay in the basement suite and make the rent payments. Why not take a step forward? Why not hop a plane and see what the Middle East has to offer a good-looking jock, albeit middle aged? Who knows what desert maidens he may entice into his tent?

And so the arrangement is made. He will fly in early October, stay a month with Ken and Sylvia and see Egypt.

Wayne survives the summer, plodding through mountain meadows while his charges photograph every wild flower and snow dappled peak that swim into view. The days are long and the wage is small and he is left with little after paying the necessary insurance coverage and re-certifying his guiding credentials. He can only hope for generous tips at the end of each three day ordeal in the wild. Europeans are best; they complain little on the trail and are big spenders once back in town, often taking Wayne to dinner at their up scale hotels. The season comes to a close as the first snows wash the high country and Wayne prepares for his journey. He has saved more than any summer before. His time in the bush has dropped his beer budget considerably and the rigours of guiding have rendered him fit and healthy despite some lingering back pain.

The bureaucracy of securing a passport has almost defeated his desire to travel and the list of inoculations has him rethinking the whole international scene. But by October 11 he finds himself checking in at the Lufthansa desk in Vancouver feeling much like a world traveller, smug in his new Dockers and fleece, surrounded by languages he is unable to identify. He surveys his fellow passengers in the waiting lounge zooming in on the single females, creating a story for each and imagining them holding a boarding pass to the seat next to his. He is familiar with the airplane fantasies: intimacy with strangers, fondling under blankets, sexual encounters in the toilet cubicles. He studies each young face hoping for some eye contact.

When he finally boards, he finds himself wedged between a middle aged Indian woman wrapped in a sari and a brooding Arab. His fantasies evaporate until the flight attendant for his cabin asks to take his daypack and store it in the overhead compartment. She smiles with a warmth he interprets as much more than professional courtesy. Her nationality is indefinable, a little Asian, perhaps Italian, or maybe one of those Middle Eastern countries he would have trouble finding on a map. It's her smile that defines her. Set in a dark complexion surrounded by dark hair. He is struck at once by her beauty and spends the first hour of the flight trying to catch her eye. He will engage her in conversation, discover where she is staying - take her for a drink. Wayne, the consummate ladies' man is pumped. When she brings him a pre-dinner beer, he catches a glimpse of her name tag, Beshka. He smiles and winks. Later, on the way to the toilet, he pops into the galley to make small talk. She stands in a striped apron sliding meals into the microwave ovens. He smiles and pitches his opening line.

"I'm Wayne, from 41 G. Anything I can do to help, Beshka?"

"Excuse me, sir, you'll have to return to your seat. We'll be serving your dinner shortly."

He detects a British accent, educated in England he decides. She gives him that same smile, enticing him to continue his pursuit.

"Is this your normal route? Where is your home base?"

"I'm sorry sir, I'm very busy just now. Could you return to your seat, please."

This response, a little more curt than the previous but still the smile persists.

"Well, it looks like you've got everything under control here. Perhaps we can chat later. I'm in 41 G next to the Hindu and the Arab."

He returns to his seat, forcing the large green sari to rise and give way. He nods to the Arab and says, "Great flight."

The Indian woman turns to him.

He is drawn to the red dot between her eyes and the heavy makeup.

"Where are you flying today, young man?"

Wayne catches the eye of Beshka as she pushes the cart up the aisle. Her firm behind speaking to him in a language he clearly understands.

"Oh, ah, Frankfurt and then on to Cairo. How about you?"

"I am on a mission to Mumbai to find a husband for my daughter."

"Oh, I see. Why do you have to travel all the way to Mumbai to find a husband? Are there no eligible young men in Vancouver?"

"In my culture one must find the right husband for one's daughter. She deserves the best, my Aradna. She is woman of my flesh; she will one day carry my grandchild and I must find the right father for this child."

"Interesting," nods Wayne, noticing the rolls of fat that have wriggled from under the waistband of the woman's sari.

"Are you married, young man?"

Wayne would like to extricate himself from this conversation but finds himself pulled to the red dot, which now seems to have taken on a life of its own.

"I was married once," he responds to the red magnet.

He is overcome with a memory of his first encounter with Laura, a girl of eighteen whose pants he couldn't wait to penetrate and did so repeatedly in the back seat of his '56 Chevy.

"Woman is special," the red dot continues, "she deserves that I should find a good man for her."

"Chicken in teriyaki sauce or beef curry?" a voice interrupts. It is not the voice of Beshka, however, but of a much older woman.

"Chicken or beef, sir?"

"Ah, chicken please." He receives the tray and strains to search for Beshka whom he notices is now plying her cart down the other aisle.

The Arab chooses not to eat. He accepts a third whiskey.

Wayne has a four hour stopover in Frankfurt. He leaves the holding area in order to wander the airport, a rambling shopping mall connected by a shuttle train. Duty free shops abound - cosmetics, cigarettes, alcohol. Wayne has been told by Ken to pick up a bottle each of rum and gin, as good liquor is impossible to find in Cairo. He complies then finds himself browsing in an adult sex outlet jammed with every conceivable aid devised for man and woman. From lingerie and lubricants to erotic literature and videos in five different languages. Wayne is transported once again into the realm of the possible. If only he could find the right woman. He is working his way through a picture book with German captions "Heidi unt Hilda..." but the text is unnecessary. The pictures tell the whole story.

His fantasy is suddenly exploded by the sound of his name on the airport speaker system.

"Passenger Lacombe. Passenger Mr. Wayne Lacombe, bound for Cairo. Please proceed to Gate C-54 immediately. This is your last call for boarding."

Wayne's arrival at the gate is met with disapproving frowns in three languages from three airline officials.

"We are just about to remove your luggage from the plane, Mr. Lacombe. You are holding up the flight and two hundred and thirty-four passengers. We have been paging you for fifteen minutes."

A matronly looking woman in full uniform is glaring down at him. He envisions a swastika on her armband, black riding boots and a whip.

His feeble apology is coldly ignored and he proceeds through the metal detector.

A buzz...

"Please empty your pockets." - some Canadian coin and three beer tabs.

A buzz...

"Please remove your shoes."

A buzz...

"Please remove your belt."

He passes through.

"Is this your backpack sir?"

"Yes."

"Please open it for me, sir."

Wayne obliges, while the security attendant carefully removes everything from the pack: two liquor bottles, a girlie magazine and his kit bag, a pair of underwear and socks. The kit bag is opened, nail clippers removed and tossed into a garbage can. The safety razor follows.

All else is returned, the security officer brandishing the magazine.

"These are not approved in Cairo, mein herr. Beware of the Islamic religious police."

Wayne apologizes to the flight attendant as he shuffles down the aisle of the crowded plane, finding his seat in the second to last row. His seatmate is a large, well-dressed man sporting rings on many fingers. A thick moustache adorns his upper lip.

"American?"

Wayne responds hesitantly. "No, Canadian."

"Oh, Canada Dry. Sit down."

Wayne collapses into his seat as the chief steward announces take off regulations and the aircraft is pulled away from the gate.

"Is this your first time to Al-Qaherah?"

"Pardon?"

"Al-Qaherah, you are going to Al-Qaherah, for the first time?"

"I'm going to Cairo. Isn't this plane going to Cairo?"

"Cairo, yes. Al-Qaherah in Arabeya."

"Oh I see," Wayne replies, while fastening his seat belt at the insistence of the flight attendant who is rushing down the aisle closing overloaded overhead compartments, eyeballing the laps of the passengers at the same time for fastened seatbelts.

Wayne imagines he is sitting beside Sadam Hussein's brother or even Sadam himself. He studies the face more closely while the man scrutinizes a newspaper. Wayne reads the headlines "Ramallah Siege Rages On". Behind the gold knuckles Wayne observes another passenger crouched in the corner. Up against the window is a black hooded figure totally draped in robes except for a narrow slit across the eyes, eyes that are staring at Wayne with curious intensity. The figure is a woman.

She quickly breaks eye contact by lowering her head. Wayne continues to stare until the newspaper drops and Sadam questions him regarding his loyalties.

"Israeli or Palestinian?"

Wayne is not really sure; he has little knowledge in current events. He feels the pressure to make some response and realizes the politically correct answer in this circumstance is Palestinian.

"I am liking Ariel Sharon more and more," states his companion.

This name Wayne has heard before. Sharon is an Israeli military big wig. But why does this man like the enemy of the Middle East?

"I am liking him because every time he kills innocent Palestinians he continues the *intifada* and the *intifada* kills the Israeli tourist economy. Nobody wants to visit Israel when bombs are exploding on the streets, so these tourists come to Egypt instead. Israel loses and Egypt wins. Ariel Sharon is now a friend to Egypt."

The covered woman beside him leans and whispers into his ear.

He turns to Wayne and asks if he will excuse his wife to visit the toilet. Wayne rises and allows the mysterious woman to pass by him and then helps her retrieve her carry on from the overhead bin.

"My wife is Syrian. I am bringing her from Damascus to my home. She is my second wife."

"Oh I see," and wants to add that she is very beautiful, but stops, realizing he has no idea what she looks like behind the mask.

Wayne takes a Heineken from the flight attendant as she wheels her cart into the back. Every second passenger looks like a terrorist. A large gentleman shuffles his way up the aisle; he is sweating profusely. Perhaps he carries a detonator inside his shirt. Behind him glides a woman of such beauty that Wayne pops his peanuts while opening the vacuum sealed bag. She is dressed like some Paris model, silk blouse, tailored skirt, hair and make-up in Cover Girl condition. She stops in front of Wayne, a vision of all that he imagined might lie in the desert oasis.

"Excuse," she speaks, "my seat."

Wayne recovers and realizes this is the wife transformed. Still girlish in her mannerisms, she replaces her carry on and slides in front of him and resumes her seat beside her husband.

Wayne follows her, transfixed, unable to remove his eyes from her flawless image until her husband pulls at his arm and he collapses into his seat.

"My wife likes to change when she is travelling on an airplane."

Wayne nods, leaning forward to catch another glimpse of the goddess by the window. She is closely studying the duty free shopping magazine periodically whispering into the ear of her attentive husband.

Wayne's expectations of the Middle East rise to a new level and he awaits with anticipation his entrance into Cairo.

Twenty minutes before landing the wife reverses her transformation and when the plane begins its descent she is draped in black as before.

As they descend, Wayne glimpses from the window, the haze of pollution and through the haze the outline of buildings in shades of grey and brown. The plane circles the pyramids before making its final approach. The huge monoliths stand like sentinels guarding this mysterious land. He watches the woman watching the pyramids through the narrow eye slits and wonders what she will make of her new home.

He follows his seatmates as they disappear into the crowd that converges on the immigration booths at the end of a long hallway.

Wayne remembers his brother's instructions, purchases the tourist visa from the wickets in front of the immigration lineups and fills out his embarkation card. Triumphal music of *Aida* reverberates through the noise and clouds of smoke as he waits and waits and waits. He reads a poster dated 1986 advertising Aida's performance at the pyramids.

Finally, he tentatively approaches the window, receives the necessary stamp and enters the country without incident. "Piece of cake," he mutters to himself.

The cake crumbles on the other side, where he is overrun by prospective taxi, limousine and bus drivers who want to transport him and his luggage anywhere. Thankfully, he is armed with his brother's catch phrase "La shokran, my driver is waiting for me," and the horde disbands.

At customs he has his passport ready.

His eye catches the passenger at the counter beside him. His bags are being thoroughly searched and expensive suits with the labels still attached are being hauled out and inspected. Wayne will find out later that importing goods in this manner is common practice. When discovered, bearers are forced to pay exorbitant taxes, sometimes more than the value of the goods themselves. He imagines what goods all the women are wearing under their draperies.

And now a commotion breaks out. There is yelling and pushing by the passenger with the tailored suits. He is tearing the clothing in front of the officers. Sleeves, lining and pockets sail over the heads of others in line, who yell and shout with a frenzy that soon draws the machine gun toting security guards towards the outburst.

"You are from Canada," a soft voice.

"Yes, I am Canadian."

"Ah, Canada Dry. Do you have anything to declare?"

"No, I don't."

"Very well. Have a nice day."

Wayne bursts through the sliding glass doors and out into the main lobby, a mass of confusion and more smoke. His brother is waving furiously, hugs and kisses him boldly on each cheek. This embarrasses Wayne to no end until he realizes every other male in the arrival hall is hugging and kissing as well.

Ken escorts him out onto the street where he has a taxi waiting. Into the haze and bustle Samir pilots his black and white Fiat, oblivious to the swarming pedestrians and other exhaust spewing vehicles.

Wayne takes a full day to recover at the flat of his brother and sister-in-law, a spacious apartment on the fifth floor of the New Osiris apartment block. On the morning of day two he explores the environs, a network of filthy streets and surprisingly green parks and boulevards. Flowering trees and poinsettia bushes protrude from the walls of private villas. The parks are fenced it appears, to keep the population and garbage out. He passes the mosque whose speakers woke him the first morning at 5:00 am. It seems empty except for the young boy laying out green mats on the sidewalk in front. The streets contain all manner of garbage, mostly the remnants of fast food outlets, McDonalds and KFC the most recognizable. Children kick deflated soccer balls in the street and call him *habibi* while women wipe parked automobiles with dirty rags and look at him with suspicion. At least he can see their faces.

He returns to the apartment, surprising a young woman with flowing hair who is damp mopping the tile floors. She drops the mop and disappears into the front room soon to reappear wearing a pale blue head covering. Wayne nods a hello and sizes her up and down. This must be the maid, Fatma, he has been told about. Not bad, he decides. He smiles and moves in to kiss her on both cheeks, a ritual he has observed many times since arriving. She steps back and holds out her hand for shaking.

"I am Fatma."

"I am Wayne, Ken's brother."

"Hello Mister. Do you want something?"

Wayne's imagination races ahead but he manages to apply the brakes. She is looking at him with mysterious dark eyes, and at the same time wanting to please him.

"Oh, ahh…coffee?"

"Aiwa, agua American?"

"Yes please."

She leaves her work, prepares Wayne a coffee, then returns to the floors. Later, she brings in the laundry from the back balcony and irons every item, socks and underwear included.

A ring at the door, answered by Fatma.

"Sabaa al khayr, Ahmad."

A thin dirty man stands with a large box on his shoulder. He enters and places it on the clean white tiles. Wayne notices this is a box of beer. "Sakara Gold" is stamped beneath the logo of a pyramid.

Fatma heads to the kitchen where she grabs several coins from a plastic cup and places them in the hand of the man. He places his hand over his heart, turns and exits.

"Beer for Mister Ken," says Fatma and she proceeds to place several green bottles in the fridge.

Wayne returns to the Egypt travel book he was given by Sylvia on day one and continues to read the Cairo section. Sightseeing will begin in earnest this weekend, when Ken and Sylvia are free from work.

He can hear Fatma busily preparing dinner in the kitchen. He stands in the doorway and watches, while she soaks vegetables in bleach water, peels potatoes and plucks two chickens. He is in awe at how much this woman has done since her arrival. He could use a woman like this back in Canada. He wonders if she is willing to travel. An exotic live-in maid, the perfect arrangement. He wonders if she belly dances.

He reaches into the fridge and removes two bottles of beer, opens them and offers one to Fatma.

She looks at him with astonishment, waving her hand.

"La. La. La."

"Go ahead, it's hot in here and you've been working so hard. I'm sure Ken wouldn't mind. Take a break. I think you and I should get to know each other a little better."

He is now pouring the beer into a glass for her, thinking that she may not want to drink out of the bottle. He takes her hand, places the glass into it and ushers her into the front room.

"Sit down and drink with me. Would you like me to play some music?"

Wayne has draped an arm around her shoulder and pulls her closer to his body.

Fatma turns away in alarm and breaks for the front door where she changes her shoes, grabs a shawl and quickly departs.

There is no dinner in the oven when Sylvia returns at 4:30 that afternoon. There is no salad in the fridge. There is no laundry folded neatly at the foot of the bed. There is no Fatma. There is only Wayne grinning sheepishly in the front room with a beer in his hand.

A telephone call from the neighbour informs Sylvia of Wayne's unsuccessful attempt to bridge the culture barrier. The maids in the building, apparently are all buzzing with the story of the rude *hawega* on the fifth floor. The neighbour's maid, who is fluent in English, has passed the story to her employer in hopes that Fatma will find some justice.

More calls by Ken to Fatma's home that evening, with and without translators eventually find Fatma willing to return to work provided Wayne is nowhere in sight of the apartment.

Followed by a long chat with Wayne about cultural differences, religious taboos and Fatma's married status, not to mention her three children. Wayne sucks it up and promises to watch himself.

"You will," says Ken, "because tomorrow you accompany me to work and on Thursday you shadow Sylvia at school."

The weekend finds Wayne astride a borrowed bicycle deep inside Waadi Digla, a desert ravine, an hour cycle from Ken's apartment. This protected area is riddled with trails, originally goat and human but now a network of mountain biking courses. The waadi is a series of plateaus beginning at the bottom where presumably a river ran thousands of years ago. From this level, trails zigzag up the canyon wall to the next level of undulating piles or rock and sand and then onto another steep incline and another.

When the three riders arrive at what appears to be the top, Wayne dismounts, drinks from his water bottle and wanders to the edge of a precipice. The wind whines faintly around him, ancestral voices of pharaonic soothsayers, he wonders. In the distance across the Nile, Ken points out the three Pyramids of Giza, and those of Sakkara and Dashur. Wayne wanders further down a spine that separates two narrow canyons and plops himself on an outcropping of limestone that hangs over the cliff. He takes another swig from his water bottle and removes his helmet.

For as far as he can see, there is nothing, no buildings, no vegetation, no signs of humanity - empty space save for brown rock and blue sky. Almost clean, he surmises, devoid of clutter and the trappings of human existence. Only me and the elements, me and this moment. Even the past seems lost in the wind that slips along the ridge. And for the first time in a long time Wayne feels something bordering on humility - the smallness of Wayne in the face of this vast emptiness. All that remains is the insignificance of who he is and the mistakes he has made, of his struggling ego and its repetitious path of peril and predictable failure.

Ken's voice interrupts his calm.

"We're ready to drop down below, Wayne. There is a box canyon out of the wind where we can have lunch."

"I think I'll just sit a bit longer, if that's okay."

"Sure, just follow the trail over that lip and you'll hit the canyon."

Wayne is left alone. A silent figure balanced on a stone above a precipice. He imagines a new life with limitless possibilities, a life scoured of its past markings like his surroundings. A hope is planted in this barren landscape, a hope that he can perhaps start again - that all the junk of his past can be stripped away leaving simply Wayne, clean and fresh and ready for a new beginning.

This was the first of Wayne's visions in the desert, although he did not realize it in the terms just described, for Wayne is a simple man and only sensed deep inside that he was feeling different here in the middle of nowhere and in spite of its peculiarity he kind of liked what he was feeling.

His second vision was to come towards the end of a journey up the Nile that Ken and Sylvia had sent him on his own. His cruise terminated at Aswan, where he boarded a small craft that motored him to Philae, an island temple to the goddess Isis. He roamed the ruins for several hours stopping for one last look at the entrance pylon that depicted the goddess Isis standing with wings outstretched.

"She is the mother, and lover of us all," a voice from behind him.

A thin man with a white skullcap and white *galabeya* approaches. Not another hawker, thinks Wayne. He has been hounded by these sellers of cheap trinkets since his arrival in this country.

"La shokran," he mouths from rote.

"She is in need of our help," he continues. "She has been forgotten. We need to listen to her voice. She has been silenced for so long," as if speaking to the stillness that haunts the island.

"The last time she was heard was at the end of the fourth century. Early Christians at that time still believed in the power of the Mother Goddess and came here to worship her. The church forbade the practice and turned the temple into the home of their Christian god, chiselling out the offensive figures of the ancient religion. Little of the goddess remains here now and her story has all but been lost."

A pause.

"She is the healer. She is the artist of life. She is the mender of broken bodies and broken hopes. Just as she resurrected the pieces of her husband, Osiris, and took him inside her to engender the father of men, Horus, she is the healer and pro-creator of all mankind."

Wayne has read the story in the travel book, how Osiris was ripped to shreds by his warring brother Seth and thrown into the Nile. How Isis collected the pieces and sewed them together, all but his penis which she could not find. In her wisdom and magic she fashioned him a phallus and brought him back to life in order to impregnate her with child.

"She is the only hope for our troubled world, a world of tension and conflict that has been fostered by men and their greed."

He could speak about the Intifada in Palestine but does not.

"Have you come to worship the mother goddess?"

"Ah, no - I'm just a tourist, from Canada."

"Ah, Canada dry!" Pause. "Ah Canada, I think your spirit has dried up. You need some drink."

He offers Wayne his water bottle. Wayne drinks long, wiping his mouth with his arm.

"I think you are a searcher. I think you have been brought here for a purpose. I think you have need of a woman to revive your spirit."

A woman, thinks Wayne, and his mind flicks through the photo album of his female conquests since adolescence, face after face of disappointed goddesses, whose bodies and souls he has disfigured in the name of selfishness and desire. In truth, he has not been listening; he has avoided all healing. He has destroyed every relationship with the goddess, every attempt to put the pieces of his life back together, every loving touch to revive his failing spirit. He has been too much "man".

He sits on a fallen granite slab and feels a wetness sliding down his cheeks. Leaning back to return the water to his strange companion, he finds he is alone, surrounded only by rock and sand and the carved etching of a woman with outstretched wings before him. The reassuring gurgle of the river echoes from a distance.

Wayne is ready to return home.

1991 - UP THE RIVER

SARAH Thompson leans poised over the long aluminum fish tank. Wayne Lacombe watches closely trying to keep his eyes on the fish while Sarah gently scoops a tangle of squirming fry, carefully turning them to indicate the black bands that run zebra like down their bodies.

"These are young coho, Wayne. Now look closely at these others in the net. There is a distinct sliver slash running the length of their bodies. They are chum fry. Notice also that when observing from above, the coho appear brown against the chum's greenish tint."

Wayne zeros in, trying desperately to distinguish between the two salmon species writhing together in the half submerged net. Sarah holds the net securely as Wayne slowly identifies coho and chum before slipping them back into the tank.

Sarah seems to be in charge here at the hatchery, having taken Wayne under her wing the minute he pulled up in his pick up truck.

The site is crawling with gum booted seniors hauling nets and buckets from the tank area to a make shift trailer. It's clipping day, he was told by Sarah when he arrived and those volunteers with good eyes and quick fingers were snipping off the adipose fins of the young coho.

Wayne knows about the process that distinguishes wild coho from hatchery fish. Four years from now anglers will be allowed to keep fish without adipose fins. Wild coho, on the other hand, are all catch and release.

"Your job, Wayne, is to separate the two species in this tank, bucket by bucket. The coho we will clip immediately and the chum you can release in the far tank next to the creek. We'll keep them for another few weeks then let them head for the salt chuck."

Wayne assumes the position and begins the scooping and separation. He is soon joined by Gordon and Hal, two old farts gowned in fishing vests and high rubber boots. Gordon holds a cigarette between his fingers. Sarah makes the introductions.

"Gordon and Hal are a couple of the originals who got this hatchery up and running back in the 50's, right Hal?"

"Fall of '56 Walter Stephenson, the owner of this farm, realized not so many fish were coming back up the creek so he and his sons hand dug all these channels to help the coho find good spawning ground."

"And that was just the beginning", continues Gordon. "DFO got involved later and the first tanks were set up in the early 60's. Now we got eight linear tanks and two round tanks with plans for more."

Gordon lifts his toque covered head and looks back up the hill toward the highway.

"All this land here is fed by springs along that hillside. We've pinpointed five but know there are more. We'll take a walk later and I'll show you where all this water comes from".

Wayne is still struggling to separate coho from chum. Gordon makes it simple.

"The long skinny ones are chum and the short fat ones are coho. Here watch me for a minute."

He deftly flips the net from bucket to bucket barely touching the slippery torsos that fall conveniently, coho to the right and chum to the left. He straightens up, almost loses his balance before Wayne steadies his girth. Gordon groans and pulls another cigarette from his vest pocket and lights it.

"I'm eighty-four this month and gettin' up and down isn't as easy as it used to be. Most of the guys here are my age. Been at it for thirty to fourty years. It's time we had some new blood here, Wayne. I hope you keep coming out."

Wayne's here because his guiding boss said they needed more volunteers at the hatchery and the more he knew about the fish business, the more he could share with the tourists who used his guiding services in the valley. Besides, it was time the sports fishing industry gave something back to the rivers.

All this Wayne understands. He is even mildly interested in the layout of spring water on the farm. But more importantly he wants to know more about Sarah. There is a quality about her. Something he has never seen in a woman, a strength and confidence.

"So, Gordon, what's with this Sarah woman? She sure seems to know her stuff."

"Oh, Sarah, she's a gem. Best thing that ever happened to this hatchery. She's been in the business for a while. University Degree and all. She's what they call an ichthyologist, a fish biologist. She's on loan from the main hatchery down island. Been with us for six months now. She's really shaped us up. Things were starting to fizzle here. Lots of morts and poor returns in the fall. We're doing a better job all round under her direction."

Wayne is amazed at the exuberance of the woman. He watches her purposeful stride, bouncing from one group of men to another, jesting and gesturing so that everyone is included in the day's operation.

When the separating is complete. Sarah invites Wayne into the trailer to watch the clipping procedure. Three-inch coho are removed from the linear tanks, dropped into a bucket of "knock down" where they are rendered lifeless, then scooped up and deposited into a series of small basins along a trough. Eight snippers stand before the basins. Fish are grabbed with tail fully exposed. Scissor blades push gently from the tail towards the head, raising the adipose fin to full extension. Then "clip"! The coho are dropped into a chute of running water, which propels them back outside and into the new round tank. By the time they hit the water they are fully revived. Sarah's voice breaks the cycle.

"Each fish takes about ten seconds to clip. The sooner we can get them back into the tanks the better. Minimal handling ensures greater survival. Out of the twelve thousand we clip today, we may only lose one or two. You want to give it a go?"

Wayne steps up to a vacated basin, lifts the scissors and begins the process. Grabbing the fish is difficult at first. He's used to handling mature fish in the river. These barely fit his palm. He soon notices that the longer he waits, the more the coho begin to revive. The more they revive, the more they squirm and the more difficult it is to expose the adipose and make the clip. Those beside him are patient with his slowness and before long he is able to keep up, even joining in the conversation and the camaraderie of the other clippers. They all have stories to tell. Stories of the big fish years when everyone caught their limit in a few hours.

Gordon has joined the line and breaks into what Wayne gathers is a story that has been shared on more than one occasion.

"Me and my buddy Otto are out in the harbor. We're in a fourteen foot boat with an inboard. We both have two lines out all at different depths. The four rods are bobbing up and down as we putt along. Otto decides he needs to take a piss. We've been drinking coffee from our thermoses all morning. He's got these damned overalls that take forever to get down but he soon hangs it over the gunnel of the boat and begins to pee."

"Well, at that moment the fish hit two lines at once. I lurch to grab one while shouting at Otto to take the other. Otto's not finished peeing yet and in his excitement he swings his body back into the boat sending an arc of piss across the exposed spark plug of the inboard motor."

"You know how water is a conductor of electricity...so that current runs right up to Otto's pecker and blows him off his feet, on to his backside and into the bottom of the boat. Well you've never seen such a look on a guy's face. He was dead white, stunned I guess. I had to yell to get him up and grab his rod before the whole thing went overboard. He didn't even put his pecker away just reefed on that reel and didn't stop winding until a lovely spring salmon broke the surface. Well we both landed our fish and went on to limit out. But from that day on Otto never took a pee over the side again."

Lots of friendly laughter even though the gang has heard the story before.

When Wayne's shift in the trailer is over he looks for Sarah, the fish woman, but she has disappeared. She's moved on to other waters, Gordon tells him. She is responsible for five hatcheries on the north end of the island.

"Take a walk with me. I want to show you my beauties."

Wayne and Gordon set out across an open field towards another branch of the river. Here a large round tank houses sea run cutthroat. Two hundred mature trout circulate in the stream filled holding tank. Wayne soon learns that this is Gordon's pride and joy. It seems he has been instrumental in developing this aspect of the hatchery."

"The cuttys are an endangered species, Wayne. If more hatcheries would do what we are doing here maybe we could start catching these beautiful trout again."

While Gordon tosses handfuls of fish feed into the tank, Wayne learns that these trout move from fresh to salt water with ease.

"They roam the entire coast of the island frequenting rivers and creeks all year round. No one really knows their migration patterns. Very little study has been done on their habits. We keep these for brood stock. Strip a few of the does for eggs and milk some bucks every spring. One of the long tanks back at the hatchery holds about three thousand fry."

On the walk back to his truck Wayne juggles the flood of fish knowledge that swims erratically in his brain, much like the recently clipped coho that now dart freely in the large green tank. He imagines the life before them when they are released into the river next spring. What dangers lurk along the journey to the sea and back.

It's several months later when Wayne is called to assist with the capture of spawning coho. He's tried on several occasions to contact Sarah but she is as elusive as the fish that frequent the pools in the river.

Wayne arrives at the oxbow in the river where the elders have gathered in circular schools garbed in hip waders and toting large nets. A sharp wind is blowing off the ocean, which quickly turns wet fingers and noses purple red. The tide is running, so the river is high and with recent rains there is enough water for the returning fish to find their way upstream.

A large weighted net has been dropped from the old bridge deck and quickly settles to the bottom, sealing off any retreat to the ocean. Upstream, a pack of beaters walk down the creek bed, nets at the ready. Gordon is amongst them, cigarette between his lips, net in the river, pushing like a snow shovel. Everyone is watching for tell tale signs, a fin perhaps or ripples.

Soon the scooping begins. Fish laden nets are passed to runners along the bank who quickly escort their catches to a large tank set on the back of a trailer.

The drama is efficiently orchestrated by Sarah who delivers orders from the bridge. She carefully scrutinizes each fish as it is wrested from the nets. Size, sex, colouring, and most importantly, wild or hatchery.

She explains to Wayne the process.

"The goal is to collect the right proportion of females to males. Females may carry up to three thousand eggs. Males, on the other hand, may have less than the desired amount of sperm. So we need more males than females. We need to guarantee that every egg is fertilized before we place them in the incubators."

Wayne is becoming mildly aroused by the sexual details slipping from Sarah's chapped lips. He has to remind himself that she is a professional and her discussion is limited to the world of fish.

Sarah returns two males who are not showing enough colour along their flanks.

"See this pink, Wayne? Without that pinkish tint any fish we haul back to the hatchery will die before breeding. The readiness is everything."

Wayne is transfixed by Sarah's flushed cheeks, the colour running all the way into her shirt collar. He manages to reconnect to the fish and Sarah's amazing story of their return to this river.

"These coho have lived two to three years in the ocean, having already spent one to two years in the river. From here we have no idea where they go. Speculation has it they leave the islands and head for deep water but no one knows for sure. There was an attempt to attach sound devices on some fish at one time with receivers established all the way up the north island to register their progress."

"What did they discover?"

"Well, let's just say there were technical difficulties and the project was abandoned."

Several smaller fish have arrived in a net, still very silver.

"Those are jacks," explains Sarah, "immature males who make the journey along with the mature run. It's Mother Nature's way of guaranteeing a high fertilization of female eggs. They don't turn pink so we'll keep those guys."

Soon the tank is full; the hip wading beaters return to their trucks and Sarah gently maneuvers the hatchery truck with its precious cargo back up the river to breeding pens where the coho will be checked each day for readiness.

Wayne wants to follow, to learn more of the mingling that goes on in the river and of the woman who makes it happen, but something holds him back. In the old days his pursuit would have been relentless, ongoing until his instincts had been satisfied. He turns his truck around and heads downstream instead, hoping to see more of the story that occurs where the ocean meets the river.

Several days later he is once again in the aura of Sarah who is firmly stroking the belly of a mature female coho. Her experienced hands slide symmetrically towards the anal opening sending a stream of pink eggs into a white bucket. Another pass of her hand is followed by another gushing of unfertilized ova. Ever the priestess, she hands the female to an assistant who returns the spent mother to the creek. A male coho is presented to her. She milks this specimen with the same controlled energy. This time a spray of grey white sperm splashes into the bucket. A second stroking produces little more.

"Very little in that buck. Bring one of the jacks. Let's see if he can muster enough to fertilize these eggs."

A small two-year-old coho is produced from one of the holding tanks and soon showers the egg bucket with gobs of milt.

"So often the case. The old males have little left after the long struggle up the river."

A few murmurs and awkward shuffling from the old geysers who stand around Sarah ready to acknowledge her every word. Gordon is the only one with balls enough to respond.

"And these young jacks have sperm to burn. Where's the justice in that?"

More groans of acknowledgement from the hand-servants of the priestess.

The bucket is raised and Sarah places her capable hands inside and begins to stir.

"This is how it all begins gentlemen. Hold your breaths and give us a silent blessing".

Just like that, thinks Wayne. She is stirring life into existence. Like some Isis of the river she is single handedly regenerating the species. She brings the gender forces together and creates life.

The process is repeated several times before there are enough fertilized eggs to fill the incubators. The donors are placed almost ceremoniously back into the river where they will soon die, giving nutrients back to the stream in which they were once nourished.

Wayne follows Sarah back to the trailer.

"Wow! That was amazing. How you handled those fish! How you mixed the eggs and sperm. You make it look so easy."

"It's not me, Wayne, it's Mother Nature's show. But if you want to know more, take this textbook. Bring it back to my office in town when you've finished and we can talk."

She is off on a mission. Her truck wheels out of the parking lot, heading for another hatchery. More fish to strip and milk. It's the time, and the readiness is all.

Over the next week Wayne peruses the text, dwelling on a few sections that capture his attention; then he finally reads the book cover to cover. He is hooked. He wants to know more about salmon and more about the woman who shapes their lives.

It's a Tuesday afternoon when Wayne appears at Sarah's office, a small cubicle in the DFO headquarters downtown. She is in mid conversation on the phone. There's been some kind of crisis at one of the hatcheries and she is talking to someone about oxygen levels in a tank full of dead fish.

"The readings need to be taken three times a day. And even then you can't guarantee against fish loss. You keep taking those readings and I'll come see you in the morning…Yeah, I'll bring a new compressor. And don't take it too hard. When we play with nature, there's bound to be a few screw ups. Yeah… You too. Bye."

Wayne has stumbled into her inner sanctum and feels awkward in the presence of a world he can barely comprehend. He fumbles for some words of greeting.

"Sorry to bother you. Sounds like you're real busy. Did they lose a lot of fish?"

"About two thousand. Months of work wiped out in one evening. Sometimes I question if we should be tampering with the natural cycle of these fish. Perhaps we should just drop all the young fry in the river, let them face the natural dangers, confront, adapt or die. Maybe in the long run we'd have hardier fish. It's not a good day to be a fish biologist, Wayne."

"I guess this is not a good time."

"So did you get through the book? A little dry eh! But an important beginning."

"Yeah. I looked at the pictures first and they got me reading. I have a few questions. Do you have some time now?"

"Not really, but if it's about salmon and you're really interested, it's worth making time. What do you want to know?"

"Well, I'd like to know more about the whole mating process. One section of the text suggests the coho mate in the river.

Another makes reference to pairs seen together in the open ocean near the estuaries. Gordon says the males go into the river first and scout the gravel then wait for the arrival of the females. The book talks about fighting for territory by mature males with jacks looming in the shadows."

"You've really done some thinking about this haven't you? Well, to tell you the truth, we don't really know. We have all sorts of theories and as many anecdotal observations but no conclusive evidence either way. The research is ongoing but there's never enough money to fund a major examination of mating patterns. We can barely manage to keep the hatcheries running let alone figure out what motivates the fish at this critical time of their lives."

"So, there's no answer? No one knows for certain what happens when the fish enter the river?"

"Not really. We have our assumptions but that's all they are. Hey! I'm going to walk the river on Thursday, from the hatchery down to the ox bow. Do you want to keep me company? We can check out the spawning channels and who knows, maybe we can add something to one of those theories."

Thursday morning is cold and Sarah arrives at the hatchery in waders, toque and a parka. A small pack is slung over her shoulder. Wayne is wearing high gumboots and his rain gear. The walk is tricky with numerous windfalls and tall grass along the banks. They avoid the creek bed as much as possible, not wanting to disturb any of the spawning fish. They are quiet for the longest time but soon the initial tension is replaced by a familiarity that only comes from long walks.

Wayne learns about the loss of Sarah's parents and her adoption by a maiden aunt who was a biology professor at UBC. She accompanied her aunt on numerous research expeditions and grew up more comfortable in a camp beside a river than in an apartment. Her best friends, in fact, are rivers and the books that she reads while sitting beside them.

Wayne is guarded about his past, revealing only that he is the product of a broken home and that he has been previously married. Sarah seems to accept it all. He even mentions his grown daughter who shares a basement suite with him in town.

They stop before noon above a large pool where several coho are holding up against the current. Sarah opens her pack and produces a bag lunch: ham sandwiches, carrot sticks, apples and a small thermos of tea. She has brought enough for the two of them.

"Gee, I didn't even think about lunch," confesses Wayne, reaching into his pocket to pull out a couple of granola bars that he adds to the lunch pile.

"No problem. Sit down here and let's watch these fish while we eat."

They chew in silence sharing the thermos of tea, staring into the pool. Sarah points out a female with three males in tow just inches behind her. Further back several jacks maneuver into place. Sarah goes on to explain.

"The females proceed up river until they find a gravel bar with just the right consistency of stones to sand and begin preparing a nest or redds as we call them. She flicks her tail fin up and down, creating a hollow in which she can deposit her eggs."

As if on cue the female begins her tail flipping ritual and the hooked nosed males move to join her. Suddenly, the larger of the males lashes out with jaws agape forcing the others to escape into the shadows.

"Now watch what happens."

With the mature males out of the picture a brave jack slides in beside the female gently rubbing his body against hers. Without warning, the dominant male returns and more biting occurs until the jack is chased off. In the meantime, the second jack has slipped into the pocket assuming the amorous role of his buddy.

"This ritual of infighting continues until the female begins to drop her eggs. Whichever male is in position at the time, releases his sperm and fertilization occurs. Sometimes it's the dominant male, sometimes it's a jack."

"So they're all fighting to be with this one woman, or female. She doesn't choose? Does the strongest and the best always win?"

"Not necessarily, it may be the male that is most adept at advancing up the river, who has conserved his strength using back eddies to assist his movement against the current. It may be a jack who succeeds because he grew faster in the river and entered the ocean a full year before the other males in his school. Notice how aggressive the mature males are, snapping and lunging at each other even the female. But there is a softness in the manner of the jacks, a gentleness that the females seems to prefer. That's my observation anyway!"

Wayne stares in wonder, first at the fish in the pool then at the red headed narrator before him. There is a long pause as each explores the mystery behind the eyes of the other. It's Sarah who breaks the spell.

"Anyway...once the female has dropped her first eggs and they have been fertilized, she moves a short way upstream and begins the process again. This time the gravel she stirs up floats downstream and covers the first redds. And so they teamwork their way up stream until they exhaust their eggs and sperm or they themselves become exhausted and drift down river to die."

It's a romantic story, thinks Wayne, a story of struggle, suffering and loss. All this, just to reproduce. And Sarah, the ruddy faced spirit before him is connected to it all. She is healing the river. She is using all the magic in her power to restore the balance of nature.

He can't help comparing the struggle of the salmon with the ease at which humans couple. A few beers, soft music and darkness. Where is the struggle there? It's all been too easy he thinks. He wonders if his love life would be any different if he had to struggle, if he had to really work at making something amazing happen.

He looks back at Sarah wanting desperately to say something honest about his feelings, to express his sense of awe and wonder at this moment. To somehow connect himself with the story of the fish. To tell her that he wants to be healed as well, that he wants to enter the sanctuary of her aura but before he can open his mouth, there is another mouth pressing against his.

It's a momentary kiss. Warm and comforting. A kiss of reassurance, of companionship with the glow of shared experience.

"Lets move on down the river, Wayne. I'm sure there's more to see, more of the story to experience."

She takes his hand in hers and they break trail along the stream heading for the ocean.

1992 - CANUDISTS

A mist inspired rainbow arches across the falls. There isn't much sun left as Wayne Lacombe maneuvers the camera, trying to capture the rainbow, the falls, the pool of water and of course, Sarah, who leans against the protective mesh, her red T-shirt rich in the long rays of the late afternoon sun. Sarah has risen from the desert of Wayne's defeated past like some Lady of the Lake, come to give him hope and renewal for the journey that lies ahead.

Wayne now strays beyond the designated path in order to take the picture, thinking, momentarily, of those film clips that show the cameraman backing off the precipice after inching his way unsuspectingly toward the cliff. The distance between them has increased considerably and he quickly checks for the edge of the rock face. The rainbow comes and goes, oscillating in the unpredictable dance of the spray. If only they would come together at precisely the same moment - the woman, the mist and the sun. He ponders at his inability to control any of the factors.

The sun drops, the rainbow disappears and Sarah turns to look at him. He takes the picture anyway and hurries back along the path, covering the distance quickly. He is in shape. Really in shape, for the first time since high school. Running regularly has been a part of his daily routine ever since meeting Sarah shortly after he returned from Egypt.

He joins her beside the truck yet somehow the distance between them remains. She has been away on course, during which time Wayne believes she has been measuring her future with him, his history, a stumbling block to any further growth in their relationship.

It has been a month since they were together and the awkwardness of their short relationship stands like the abyss between him and the falls. But somewhere in between there is a rainbow and somewhere inside there is joy.

"My heart leaps up when I behold a rainbow in the sky" suddenly surfaces from some memory work in a high school literature class. Mr. McIntyre made them memorize the opening line from every major work they studied - some theory he had about opening lines. Wayne recalls the line but not the theory.

"Hungry?"

They motor through the park munching on zucchini bread she has prepared for the trip. Wayne can tell that the canoe has shifted by the way the ropes alter from tight to loose. When not watching the potholes, he watches the ropes and when not watching the ropes, he watches Sarah.

She reads from the park guidebook.

"The shores of Azure Lake are generally steep and along some parts, waterfalls flow off of the abrupt escarpment. The most notable waterfall is the seventy-five foot Rainbow Falls, situated where Angushhorne Creek approaches the lake..."

Wayne punctuates the ensuing commentary with jokes, mostly sensual. He likes her reaction, a small grin masked by the rusty blonde hair that has fallen forward as she reads. He watches her closely as she returns to the guidebook. There is a strength and beauty about her and her beauty is more now, away from the hot city and away from the other vacationers who haunt the highway attractions.

She is close to home here, a wood nymph dressed in hiking boots, shorts and ball cap. She is coming alive. He watches her, natural and clean, yet with a sparkle of mischief in the smile that responds to his suggestive talk. She laughs and giggles her way through the next entry while Wayne runs his hand along her leg and under the hem of her shorts.

"In 1933, John Bunyan Ray came to the lake shore with his bride Alice Ludkey, built a cabin and cleared land for a small farm. Their first child was born in the late fall of 1934 in nearby Little Fort. In January, with two feet of snow concealing the trail, mother, father and infant safely made the return journey home, to what is now called Ray Farm."

Wayne contemplates the meaning of "home". He has been living in a basement suite ever since his wife left him. Although his landlords, Ted and Jean, have protected him like the child they never had, for Wayne, the Dawson's suite has never felt much like a home. The dream of some land and a real home rises from some deep longing.

The boat launch is beyond the campsite they soon pass and after some organizing of supplies, they ease the yellow fiberglass canoe into the clear green water.

It is nightfall when the canoe finally touches sand several miles down the lake. The sound of a creek and the pale shadow of the beach direct them to a narrow piece of sand with barely enough slope to lay a sleeping bag between the lakeside cedars and the water itself.

Candles appear from deep inside one of the secret caches in Sarah's pack. She carries the sun with her, he muses, struggling to ignite some driftwood into flames. By the time the fire is a success, she has unloaded the canoe, prepared the dinner and laid out the sleeping bags. The mysteries of her backpack kitchen intrigue him. Wayne is no stranger to the backcountry having guided curious foreigners along mountain trails and quiet waterways. On these overnight ventures, however, he has relied on prepackaged food and simple snacks.

From Sarah's pack, exotic spices come forth, along with oysters, noodles, onions, and potatoes. While Wayne stirs the stew and Sarah nurses the foil cooking, they both sip a white wine, tastefully served in wine glasses that have also miraculously emerged from the magical blue pack. He has nicknamed her the "practical romantic". He wants to be closer.

It starts to rain. Dinner is cleared away and the two of them scramble to protect the remainder of the gear before seeking shelter in the trees. They huddle close together under the cedars, comically positioned against a stump, their ensolites providing some protection from the damp ground. The brief shower becomes a stereophonic thunderstorm. In semi-sleep they plan their strategy.

It pours. They build a makeshift shelter using the overturned canoe and random pieces of poly. Lightning strikes a tree on the opposite side of the lake and the two of them stare with wonder at the burning torch that has now totally illuminated the far shore. He watches her watching the sky, red hair wet and clinging to her forehead. Undisturbed and unshaken she is enjoying this display of nature's own candlesticks. She turns and hugs him, her wet lips touching his. They lick each other's faces and for a moment, a seriousness overcomes her. Wayne looks inside her eyes and discovers an honesty that is both innocent and mature. He longs to belong to this child woman whose secrets he is only beginning to unveil. Sarah pulls him toward the overturned canoe.

The candles that she has placed on the underside of the seats faintly reveal the sleeping bags, brown on bottom, blue on top. In the damp flickering light they make love and for a moment Wayne feels closer. Inside her body he is approaching the source of her mystery and for a moment he feels greater than himself, greater than the water that lies only a few feet from his body, greater than the rain that thunders down on the canoe and greater than his past that clings to him like old skin.

He holds her tightly, hoping to freeze the moment, tears beginning behind his eyes. The candle, suffocated by its own wax, goes out and the darkness rushes in.

The heat of mid morning forces them out from under the canoe and into the cool clear water. Dropping the last of civilization's ties on the beach, the two bodies break through the surface; he, breast stroking away from the shore, she, crawling with ease, parallel to the beach. He stops to watch the power and strength in her movement, the natural flow of her body through water.

Suddenly Wayne feels a turning in the water and a force propels him towards that power. Diving under the water, all becomes blurred, the stones, the fish-like shapes of submerged wood, the silver glint of sand. He surfaces and there she is, beside him, clean, fresh and alive. His whole body tingles and aches. Something has been washed away - his failures, his disappointments, the uncertainties, the blundering ego that has guided him for so long.

They kiss. He holds her buttocks and traces the curve of her hips. It all feels so right. And everything is turning. Something is moving inside of him. It comes and goes. He feels the pieces slowly coming together - the water, the sun and the woman.

The bar of soap that he had left on the stone by the beach is now in his hand and he is touching her, gently brushing her soft skin. Fingers on cheeks, lips, tickling ear lobes stroking her neckline. There is no resistance. The soap slips between her small taut breasts and disappears below the surface. His hand follows. She shudders and presses herself against him, rubbing his chest against the slippery surface of her breasts. Her hair shines in the brilliance of the sun as she arches her head in laughter. The sound echoes like ripples on the lake.

She is the water; she is the sun, and he, in his clumsiness has touched them all. Without warning she slips beneath the water, vanishing like a rainbow, leaving nothing but a soap trail of bubbles.

In his new awareness, Wayne staggers to the shore and throws himself down in the hot sand. He feels complete, and at the same time free and secure. With this woman and in his place he has been transformed. He sits before this embodiment of Isis who plays before him, plunging and surfacing like some water sprite.

Beneath his hands a veritable jewelry box of semi precious pebbles lie glinting in the brightness of the morning. He scoops a hand full of white, green and reddish pearls and studies them in the sunlight. He plucks a perfect oval and discards the rest. The wine dark stone is flawless and when he licks its surface the colour assumes a richness and depth that makes him pocket the gem in order to hold its beauty. Sarah emerges from the water, droplets glistening on her fair skin.

"How 'bout some breakfast? It's my turn."

"Sure, I'll pick some blueberries to put in the pancakes."

Before he can rekindle the fire, she is dry, in shorts and blending into the cedars.

"Hey, Sarah, where's the pancake mix?"

"In the blue pack, in the flashlight pouch, next to the popcorn."

"How you doin'?"

"Great. There's some huge ones back here."

The warmth of her singsong response runs along his spine and into his shorts. Gone is the awkwardness and distance. They are together.

"Sorry, but this mix is awfully lumpy."

"Would you quit saying 'sorry'. It's looks just fine. Here, pour one and add some of these."

The berries float in the milky batter, refusing to dissolve. She smiles with purple stained lips. Wayne folds the pebble into the palm of her hand, squeezes and kisses her knuckles.

"A gift for the goddess. I have so little to offer you."

She smiles, almost tearfully, turns and gently secures the offering in the magical blue pack.

"A a a lee luuuu ja a a!"

"Aaaaaaa leee lu ja!"

Their voices bounce across the water like skipping stones. She has taught him this musical round with all its ups and downs. He is still having trouble distinguishing all the ups from the downs, often purposely, for the laughter it produces in her warms his spirit.

The journey continues, down the lake, past the old Ray Farm where the incoming creek turns them crazy and hurls them in spasms of laughter on to the sand until the sun's shadows stretch across the portage and they can laugh no more.

The light comes and goes. For four days they chase each other's hearts and bodies across the water, through the trees and up and down the beach. The light comes and goes. And with the passing of each day, the healing of Wayne continues.

This is the natural rhythm I have been so long without, he thinks. This is Sarah's rhythm and he hopes this rhythm will also be his for as long as the goddess is with him.

1993 - THE RIVER STYX

WAYNE Lacombe squeezes the spit valve on his aged trumpet and blows forcefully, sending a fine spray of water onto the mildewed carpet at his feet. He looks across to the flute section and catches Sarah's eye; a small grin escapes from her puckered lips.

It's been more than a year now since he found her, or rather she found him and he still can't believe his good fortune. They've settled into the warmth of mutual companionship sharing most of their free time. They have roamed the hills, kayaked the coves and islands and cycled the back roads of the valley. Wayne remains in his basement suite, Sarah in her apartment. Nothing has been said regarding shared accommodation in spite of Ted and Jean's encouragement to pursue this woman with all intensity.

"What's the matter with you, Wayne? You have to make a move on this woman before she slips away. Get in there and pop the question. She is the 'one'!"

"Now Wayne, Sarah is such a lovely girl and we think she would make you very happy. She is just what you need in your life. If there is anything we can do to help this relationship along, please let us know."

At Jean's insistence the four of them dine together on Sunday evenings with amiable conversations that secretly promote marriage, family and home. Wayne bites his lip and smiles awkwardly at Sarah.

Joining the community band was Sarah's idea; they needed to get out and socialize she suggested. And so he dusted off the horn that had been stored for years deep in his closet, the horn that his parents had purchased second hand when he entered junior high school and blew faithfully until grade eleven. All the music stopped that year, his father leaving home and his mother withdrawing from the world.

"Bar seventeen, are we starting at bar seventeen?"

Bryce Atkins shares the third trumpet stand with Wayne. He is in his eighties, still blows a mean horn but can't hear a thing, including the conductor's directions. Wayne acts as hearing aid and echoes all the director's instructions in full voice.

"No, Bryce, bar seventy!"

"Bar seven?" Pause. "There's no bar seven marked on the music."

"Bar SE-VEN-TY! – seven zero, Bryce."

"Oh, seventy, that makes sense. That's where we just stopped."

The music resumes with Bryce blasting the notes that march across the page in front of him. He reads well, observed Wayne after the first rehearsal but has no sense of dynamics. Everything comes out forte.

The band wheezes to a halt as director Beth, a young woman with patience beyond sainthood, alerts the band to the dynamic markings at bar seventy.

"Look at your music, at bar sixty-eight there is a sforzando followed by a decrescendo for two bars. By bar seventy we are at mp, mezzo piano."

"What's she say? Why doesn't she speak up? She's too timid to be a director."

Bryce has seen the coming and going of nine directors in his thirty-seven years with the band and compares them all with the last great director who stepped down the year his hearing started to fail. Everyone since has failed to meet his expectations.

"Mezzo piano, Bryce. Bar seventy is mezzo piano."

"Oh, softer, you mean."

"Right."

Wayne raises his eyebrows and smiles across the music stands to Sarah. They play this eye contact game throughout rehearsals holding the connection for as long as possible before eye hopping back to the music.

Beth raises her baton and all forty-three musicians launch into the remaining bars of the overture. However, an obstacle that looms between bar eighty-six and the finale raises its ugly head.

DC al coda the music reads.

Wayne, in mid phrase, wracks his brain for the meaning of the acronym. DC...DC...his imagination runs wild. Delay Conclusion - Don't Continue - No! It's something Italian - Domine Caprio.

But it's too late. The band has hit the DC and gone somewhere else in the piece of music. Wayne flounders, searching the chart for anything familiar. Bryce tootles on unaware of Wayne's confusion.

Beth's hands drop, orchestrate a disgusted wave, and the band stops.

"Sounds like most of you missed the sign...again!"

"What line?" queries Bryce.

"The sign!" bellows Wayne.

"I followed the sign. It means return to the beginning and play through to the coda. It's called Da Capo."

"Thank you Bryce. At least someone is reading his music. Let's try it again from bar 70 and follow the road map. If you don't know where you are going, draw a pencil line to help."

Wayne borrows Bryce's pencil and scribes a wavy line from the bottom of the page to the top and another from one coda sign to the other coda sign at the bottom of the page.

Beth raises her arms and the ensemble launches into the final strains before hitting the sign, leaping to the beginning on down to the coda, hop scotching to the next coda and into the last bars of the maestoso.

The swelling finale, with horns blaring and percussion pounding, continues to reverberate around the small room as the group disbands for its evening break. But not before the president has a few announcements.

"We are on for Nov.11, at the War Memorial in front of the Legion. How many will not be able to attend?"

"November 7th?" Bryce voices from the back row.

"November 11th, Remembrance Day!"

These last lines are delivered in unison by the entire band at a defenseless Bryce who musters his well-honed response.

"She'll just have to learn to speak up!"

"Good, all we need is a few instruments from each section. Beth has selected a march and two hymns. Greg will blow the last post and reveille as he did last year."

"Will they feed us afterwards?" a voice from the tuba section.

"There will be coffee and perhaps some cakes."

"Not like the old days!" uttered by a weathered face clutching a saxophone.

As the others rise to stretch or walk the hall to the bathrooms, Bryce sits reminiscing, his watery eyes lost in the dripping wet of a cold November long ago.

"In the old days after the service, we used to retire to the Legion for hot rums, then sit massaging the mugs with our red hands while remembering the men who never returned."

Wayne crouches beside him longing to join Sarah but realizing Bryce needs to tell his story.

"We used to march in those days...smart in our blue blazers, all the way down main-street to stand in front of the cenotaph. Didn't even use music. Had it all memorized. Now we're relegated to the back, draped in our mismatched rain slickers looking like refugees. Half the band won't even turn up. Too wet or too cold, they'll say. Hell, one year we played in the snow. Huge wet flakes dropping on the wreaths while old Jack Thomas blew the last post. Now there was a horn player. I got to play it one year but nothing like Jack. He died a few years back."

Sarah has joined Wayne and Bryce and responds to the last words.

"Bryce, do you need a ride to the War Memorial this year? We have room in the truck."

"Well, I was thinking I might not go. Sometimes I feel the band doesn't really need me anymore." A long pause. "But if you're offering a ride, I'll take you up on it."

Next week there is a vacant chair beside Wayne and the whole rhythm of the evening is out of whack. He's come to rely on Bryce's idiosyncrasies to marshal his own performance. He counts poorly, misses a few entrances, and fails to match pitch with the rest of his section.

Bryce's loud vocal counting of rest bars has given Wayne a confidence that he realizes is rooted entirely in Bryce's presence. Without Bryce tonight, Wayne is on shaky ground.

At the break, the president announces that Bryce has suffered a stroke on the weekend and is presently in hospital. Although he remains paralyzed on his left side, he is coherent and up for visitors. A card circulates throughout the band and Wayne signs-

Looks like you've been side tracked by a coda sign, hope you find your way back soon. P.S. I can't count without you. Cheers, Wayne

Returning home in his truck, Wayne suggests to Sarah that they try to get in and see Bryce before he leaves the hospital for home.

"I don't think Bryce will be going back home. He lives alone, you know, and he won't be able to take care of himself adequately considering his paralysis. Bev, in the flute section, says he will have to go into a nursing home, probably Mountain View."

Wayne ponders the thought of living the rest of one's days at Mountain View. He knows the labyrinth of hallways and the caverns of the living dead that occupy that venerable institution overlooking the valley and the mountains beyond. He struggles to picture Bryce retreating into its bowels, withdrawing from the light of day.

"We'd better go see him tomorrow after work."

The visit is awkward. Bryce insists he will be going home, that he is more than capable of looking after himself and the band better not give his chair up to someone else. He'll be coming back. He speaks with a contorted face, one half static, the other overcompensating. Wayne has brought him a cassette tape of trumpet concertos. They help him into a wheel chair and spin along the corridors to the cafeteria. They sit in silence as the coffees cool.

"Are they taking good care of you, Bryce?"

"Goddamn people in my room are yelling all night long. Can't sleep. Will be glad to be in my own bed soon."

"Is there anything you need from home, Bryce?"

"Bring my music in. I want to go over my parts. And my mouthpiece. I need to keep my lip muscles in shape."

Sarah wipes the dribbles from Bryce's face as he struggles to sip his coffee. His embouchure is shot realizes Wayne. Poor Bryce is incapable of gripping the rim of a cup let alone a trumpet mouthpiece.

Fall turns to winter and Bryce, as predicted, is ensconced in Mountain View at the recommendation of health officials. In mid December, the band plays a short concert of seasonal tunes in the recreation room at the home. Bryce sits alone in a wheelchair at the back of the room looking anything but entertained. Beth, the band director, acknowledges Bryce's association with the community band.

"Our next number is dedicated to Bryce Atkins. Bryce played his first concert with this band in 1954. As a matter of fact he was one of the original members who came together in that year to make music for the community he loved. Concerts, dances, parades, Bryce attended them all for thirty-seven years. His brassy trumpet has been quiet since last fall and we in the band have missed the sound of his bellowing voice as he counts the measures between entrances. He has kept us all in time over the years and reminds us of the importance of dedication and commitment. For Bryce we now play 'The Bugler's Holiday'."

When the three solo trumpeters return to their chairs a sudden drum roll followed by a cymbal crash triggers the miraculous appearance of Santa Claus from the percussion section. Ray Townsend, possibly the slimmest band member on record, garbed in the traditional red and white, waltzes from the rear of the band guided by the melodic strains of "Here comes Santa Claus". The crowd displays a noticeable recognition of the jolly old elf and a few souls clap their hands to the rhythm of the music. Ray laughs and "Ho's" his way around the room depositing candy canes in the laps of the residents, candy canes that are quickly removed by sharp-eyed nurses versed in the diet restrictions of their charges.

The band closes with "Silent Night" and those same nurses parade candles through the semi darkness whispering the time-honored lyrics.

"Sleep in heavenly peace, sleep in heavenly peace."

Tears accompany the singing of those who sit in wheelchairs awaiting the coming of the final darkness.

Following the concert the women's auxiliary provides tea and tarts. Sarah and Wayne try to engage Bryce in conversation but have little success. When the goodies have all been consumed and the music stands loaded into pick up trucks, they wheel him down to the room he shares with three others. His privacy is sparse, a bed, a dresser and a recliner. While Wayne helps him from the wheel chair Sarah peruses the photos displayed on the dresser. Metal-framed portraits from the war years, parents, a brother shot down over France.

"Where is this photo taken, Bryce?"

Bryce slowly swivels in his recliner and focuses on a treed landscape taken somewhere along the river.

"My place."

"Your place?"

Bryce is swimming back to a time before his decay and collapse. His face is changing even in its rigid paralysis. A softness comes over his eyes as he returns to youth and the promise of dreams. Sarah has hit the target; Bryce rises to the bait and gushes forth the truth of his former life.

"Mother and Dad bought it when we first came to the valley. Always hoped to build next to the river. Could never quite afford it. Held on to the land though. Built a small shack with a cot and a wood stove. William and I used to inner tube from the riverbank down to the estuary and hitchhike back. We'd fish for hours in the fall, share our catch with neighbors in town. Sometimes we'd take girls out and camp. Will was a bit of a ladies' man. There was a lively redhead he was partial to, I remember...Fred he used to call her...Freddy...short for something. She was some gal. He probably would have married her, but the war came along...when Will never came back, I was forced to spend most of my time with the family business. I'd camp for a week out there now and again. I even invited the girl named Fred to come along, which she politely did, once, but it wasn't the same without Will. Then she moved on. After the folks died I used to go out once a year in the fall to fish but there was no joy in camping alone. Haven't made the trip for years. Kids have probably vandalized the place by now."

"Seems beautiful, Bryce. We should all go take a look some day!"

"Great idea, Sarah. Some warm spring day we'll come pick you up, go for a drive and check out your property, Bryce. What do you say?"

"Better than sitting in this cell block, waiting to die."

Early March sees willow fur turn yellow and the first sticky poplar buds fill the air with spring aftershave. Run off has swelled the river into a churning foam of white curls. Wayne and Sarah carefully unload Bryce from Wayne's pick up and bundle him into the wheelchair. They roll along a well-worn fisherman's trail beside the river and soon pass a cabin in partial ruin.

"Stop here and watch the water!" a command from Bryce.

Bryce stares into swirling eddies, fumbling for some memory. When he has uprooted it, he orders Wayne to find three sticks which he then struggles to distribute.

"Roll me closer and we throw together."

Clutching a piece of cedar in his good hand Bryce stretches his arm back and sends the twig out into the current just above a small set of rapids. Wayne and Sarah's sticks splash close behind.

"Now push. Keep up with the boats."

And the race is on. Wayne leans into the wheelchair and increases the RPMs. Sarah bounds along in front of them, cheering on the boats. Bryce, now animated, has slipped into childhood and hollers into the foaming water.

"Come on cedar! Help me river. Lift me over rocks. Carry me to the sea!"

Leaders change quickly. Sarah's sleek cottonwood branch moves ahead downstream but gets hung up in a back eddy. She screams into the spring air.

"Let me free! Let me go!"

Bryce's cedar bark jets forward and sprints down an angry rivulet, out distancing Wayne's chunky fir splinter. Sarah's craft is finally released and after finding a major current, soon rejoins the race. But the cedar is in trouble, wedged at the bottom of a long chute of rapids, only to bounce up and into a narrow fissure of rock where it jams completely. Sarah takes the lead with Wayne bobbing behind.

"It's you and me now, Big Boy."

"I hope so, I've been hoping so for some time now. Lash me to your speedy craft and let's tumble together down the river, oblivious to the torrents around us."

Wayne is impressed with this brief outpouring of poetic metaphor but cannot continue. They have come to the end of the trail and a large rock bluff stands before them. They watch the two remaining sticks for as long as possible but not before Sarah's disappears under a sweeper that reaches out into the river. It fails to resurface.

"Looks like I'm the winner, Sarah. Doesn't always pay to be the fastest, you know. So what's my prize?"

Sarah smiles a pixie grin and kisses him hard on the mouth. Wayne encloses her in his arms not wanting to let her go.

"It's picnic time. You start a fire and I'll get the sandwiches from the truck."

Sarah sprints away kicking her heels. Wayne, with the old grin firmly etched on his face, turns to Bryce.

"Isn't she something else?"

Bryce has fallen silent, slumped back into the wheelchair, exhausted from his last journey on the river.

"Want to take a look at your old cabin, Bryce. See what's left?"

Bryce murmurs something inarticulate, his face contorted. He is motionless slipping away into the past.

"Sarah, come back. Something's happened to Bryce."

Sarah races along the path, picnic supplies bouncing off her hips until she crouches beside the wheelchair out of breath.

"Bryce, Bryce, smile for me. Try to smile. Say something!"

Nothing.

"Bryce, can you raise your arm? Try to raise your arms."

A small movement in his right arm, a gesture that she is being heard.

"Bryce, stick out your tongue for me. Pretend you're blowing your trumpet."

A bubble oozes between Bryce's lips and on down his chin.

At the emergency room, Bryce is thoroughly examined and hospitalized. Wayne and Sarah see him settled and sedated in a ward on the third floor. They make their goodbyes, Wayne with a hand squeeze and Sarah a gentle kiss on his cheek. Together they walk the halls holding hands not speaking, out to the truck and home. They hug for a long time on Sarah's front steps.

"I love you, Wayne. Please stay with me tonight."

At work the next day, Wayne is informed of Bryce's death. He suffered a massive stroke in the early morning. Wayne later learns that a distant relative from Vancouver is handling the funeral arrangements and will be acting as executor. Wayne contacts him and inquires about a service for Bryce.

At the funeral home Wayne blows the last post, barely controlling his tears. Six months later, after the estate is settled, Wayne and Sarah purchase Bryce's property. They plan to build a cabin on the river.

1994 - LET IT RUN

THE dragon boat eases from the dock and swings out into the harbour. Wayne Lacombe is standing at the till. Nineteen women reach and pull in front of him. One of them is Sarah.

Wayne is here at Sarah's request. The regular tiller has been side lined with a shoulder injury since June and steersmen are hard to find in the valley especially for the Angels Abreast dragon boat team, a crew composed primarily of cancer survivors. Sarah is here in support of the cause; she lost her aunt to breast cancer two years ago.

The boat is gliding in full flight now past the breakwater that protects the sailboats of the wealthy and on to the wharves that are home to the commercial fishing fleet.

"Let it run."

Paddles come out the water and while Wayne holds the boat steady in the current of the changing tide, the women work through a series of stretching exercises ending with partners facing and gently leaning into each other's clasped hands.

"This reminds us that we are connected to one another," says coach Diane.

"No matter what, we pull together. We hang onto each other to the end of the race."

There is one vacant seat today. Bernice has been re-diagnosed after being cancer free for three years. She is undergoing chemo and too weak to join the team on the water tonight. Janice pushes her hands against the emptiness where Bernice would normally sit.

Wayne watches it all from his perch at the stern, waiting for the command to take the ladies out further, away from the traffic entering and exiting the harbour mouth. A light wind has come up and a small chop rocks the boat as paddles are raised in unison and plunge together.

Wayne surveys the water ahead alert for driftwood and patches of seaweed, always conscious of the water depth. Shallows appear suddenly when out of the main channel and strict observance guarantees the safety of the women who strain in front of him. Several he knows are non-swimmers and become easily unsettled whenever they cross the wake of a powerboat or turn quickly into the wind.

Diane calls for some practice starts - six plus sixteen. Six powerful strokes to get the boat going, followed by sixteen increasingly faster strokes. This is race season and getting off the start line in good time will be essential at the festival down island next weekend.

Wayne barks the commands that start every race.

"Attention paddlers. We have a line."

Wayne mimics an ailing air horn and nineteen paddles pull against the dead water. The first few strokes seem futile. Moving this barge of a boat off the start line is no easy feat. By the end of the first six, the elastic grab of the water is broken and the boat surges forward. At 'sixteen' Wayne hollers "Let it run" and the boat coasts gracefully through the water.

Diane calls for a post mortem - not the best choice of words with this group.

"Timing is an issue", reminds Diane, "as we accelerate to race pace. All paddles must enter the water at the same time. Always watch the top hand of the leads."

Sitting in the front row, the leads, Cindy and Rayanne, are responsible for setting the pace, slow enough to allow everyone to endure the five hundred metre course yet fast enough to maintain a race speed. They are both veterans and have worked their way up the boat to this prestigious position at the bow. In the rear sit the newbies, where the water has been churned and re-churned by the nine rows ahead. Paddling here is a challenge and correct technique critical. Everyone starts off in the stern.

It's "paddles up" again with twenty strokes to get the boat going. The zigzag drill is next. Front left and back right paddle together followed by front right and back left. This keeps the boat moving while giving a rest to half the crew. Wayne steers towards the spit, a treed finger that thrusts into the bay creating a narrow opening before the rough water of the strait. The spit will provide some protection from the southeast wind, that is now creating cat's paws on the wave crests.

"Let it run."

The women drink from water bottles; some remove a layer of clothing. Paddling a dragon boat is hard work and not for the faint of heart.

The women talk now between drills, some commenting on a new development on the fore shore, others identifying wild fowl that constantly land and take off. The newbies in front of Wayne want to know more about Bernice, the missing paddler. Bernice is responsible for recruitment and the reason they are here. She speaks often at breast cancer clinics and has emerged as the motivational voice in the valley, continually confirming that there is life after cancer. She is the hero of Angels Abreast.

Diane repeats what she has heard regarding Bernice's biopsy. Yes, the cancer has returned, this time in the left breast. First they will treat with surgery, then chemo, followed by massive radiation. Bernice is in good spirits and plans to rejoin the team for the season opener at the lake next spring.

There is a silence in the boat. The cancer survivors know the story only too well. They have fought this battle and realize they may have to fight again. There are no clear winners in the cancer race. Just when one thinks they have triumphed, the old foe reappears and the struggle begins all over again.

Sarah twists and looks back at Wayne. She knows how he hates this ongoing conversation.

"Why can't we just paddle?" he will query in the truck on the way home. She listens to Diane's reassurance to the others that Bernice will be back. Sarah recalls her aunt's final days in hospital and wishes the dragon boat experience had been part of her therapy. Facing the uncertainty of cancer is not the time to be alone, she realizes.

Rest is over and the paddlers switch from left to right and right to left. This is an awkward maneuver for many of the women. Some rise and step across the boat while their partner slides along the narrow seat.

"Brace the boat."

All paddles lay flat on the water as the tricky procedure begins.

They run the next drill along the shallow water of the spit. Sand dollars and oysters punctuate the bottom of the clear water. This is what Wayne enjoys. A light breeze in his face, he weaves between anchored sailboats as the ladies follow the ripple drill, row after row picking up the rhythm of the boat. A seal breaks the surface off the port side and stares at this nineteen-finned monster bearing down. It slips under and disappears. An eagle starts a long approach to an old piling, stalling just before its claws catch the weathered post and collapses its wings. It's great to be alive, muses Wayne as he turns the boat for home. Inching his way along the breakwater, he catches a reflection of the crew in the calm of the water. Heads and bodies and arms all leaning and pulling in unison like some strange creature propelled by forces beneath the surface that no one can control. Wayne lifts the tiller from the water and the boat continues forward without his interference. He closes his eyes and feels the slow pulsation of the boat through his feet and legs. He opens and closes his eyes periodically as the boat nears the dock. He calls a final "let it run" and the boat nudges against the rubber tires on the dock.

"Thank you Wayne." the ladies echo as they are pulled from the boat to the dock by Diane's trusting arm.

Down island it's race weekend and the tent village beckons the Angels Abreast as they descend from the parking lots above the waterfront. Ninety teams are in attendance, some coming from as far away as Seattle and Portland. Most teams are not cancer survivors as the sport has grown exponentially and now includes mixed teams and women's teams. Cancer survivor teams make up the smallest group, twelve at this event.

There is a festive atmosphere in the tent village. Two thousand athletes in all sizes and shapes have come together to compete on friendly terms. To Wayne, the competition seems secondary, most are here for camaraderie and the ongoing social events: early morning stretches, pancake breakfasts, displays from various suppliers and of course the beer tent where everyone converges at the end of the day.

The team checks out the T-shirts with fire breathing dragons emblazoned on the chest, the official festival logo. Wayne finds himself checking out a few chests himself. Team names have no boundaries. "Paddle Pushers", "Aquaholics", "Blazing Paddles". On the back of one shirt he reads, "Paddling makes us wet". He sips a coffee and wanders down to the marshalling area where as a tiller he will be given race instructions including the start calls. Tides are tricky at this venue and the wind can make the lining of four boats at the start more than challenging. The last thing a race official wants is a false start. Backing up four, fifty-foot tubs is no picnic, especially in wind and waves. The calls are established. "Attention paddlers, I have a line," followed by an air horn, easily heard if down wind but barely audible above. The meeting disbands with questions regarding the loading and unloading of boats.

The first race finds Angels Abreast in boat number four, the outside lane of the racecourse. This is an unfavourable spot that takes the first full impact of the prevailing winds. The chop is excessive as the boats make the wide turn at the start line. The starter, bobbing in a light, aluminium skiff, megaphone to his lips, is barking orders to the tillers.

"Boat two...move to the start line. Boat one...hold hard! Boat four...turn into the wind and hold!"

Wayne is struggling to keep the boat in position but the tide is pushing him closer to the starting buoy. He wishes the starter would call "alignment" so they can get the race underway and just as he nudges the buoy the air horn goes.

It's a poor start with paddlers on the left side unable to get good water on their paddles, the buoy impeding their forward thrust. Once out in the open, the boat picks up pace as the ladies lean and rotate into the pattern they have rehearsed ad nauseam. The caller, a young woman, daughter of Bernice, encourages the team.

"Long and strong. REACH. Come on Angels! Pull together."

Five hundred metres is a long haul for the team. Wayne is required to overtill in order to keep the boat on track. Wind and tide play havoc with line. A powerboat races by, sending wash against the gunnels of boat four but the women are undaunted, stroking together until the finish line is crossed by the head of the dragon mounted on the bow.

All is spent. Gasps of exhaustion.

They finish last but with a respectable time. Diane is pleased.

"Well done, Angels. That was our best time this year. 2:53. That should place us in the Jade Division where we can possibly win a medal."

At noon the team parades down the causeway bearing paddles and pink carnations. This is a traditional ceremony to honour those who have fallen to the dreaded disease. An arch of raised paddles leads the pink ladies to the water where they stand in reverence while words of encouragement from cancer survivors float over the assembly of bowed heads. A song of hope, familiar to these women, echoes across the water from some portable speakers as the carnations are tossed into an ebbing tide.

The flower heads hang lifeless in the pulsating waves, each carrying the memory of a lost friend and a reminder that the possibility of an early death is but one doctor's visit away. By the end of the day these pink faces will be washed out to sea, gone in all but memory.

The women return to their tent. A quiet sobriety has descended upon them and it's all Diane can do to raise their spirits for the afternoon's finals. Wayne stands outside the warm up circle, unsure of how he fits into this drama. He wishes Sarah were here to make sense of this emotional cocktail. To lose a breast is beyond his understanding but to lose a loved one touches something deep inside, a scar that he has done everything to cover with layers and layers of bravado and swagger. Since meeting Sarah, the layers have been disturbed and the wound of his first failed love has resurfaced despite his attempts at repression.

The race is called and the women assemble at the starter's gate. The team cheer lacks the passion of the morning; nevertheless, the boat is loaded and Wayne steers the craft out into the receding tide.

The day ends badly for Angels Abreast. Dawn sits out the next two races complaining of a strange soreness in her shoulder. Even Diane stops paddling in the last race. She explains it as a cramp but some of the women know she has been hiding pain for some time. The Angels fail to medal, but the ladies show no remorse. They raise their beer glasses in the Dragon's Lair and drink to the success of the season.

Wayne is frustrated with the team. They insist on leaving vacant seats for those who are ill or have recently died. Today, a pink life vest was strapped into row three where Fiona had sat for seven seasons. When Wayne questioned the logic of this decision he was quickly rebuffed by Bernice's daughter.

"Fiona was a founding member of the Angels and her death reminds every one of us of our mortality."

Wayne argues that racing without a full contingency makes competition difficult and the untrimmed boat pulls unnecessarily to one side or the other. He refuses to curb his disappointment as they load their gear heading for home.

"How do you expect to win or even place without a full boat of paddlers? There's no way this team will ever be competitive."

Diane's response still echoes in his mind.

"Wayne, this is not about competing. This is about surviving."

1995 - EARLY FALL

THE snow can be heard from inside the tent; the gentle contact with the tarp and the constant drip onto the fly suggest a cold wet sleet. Temperatures must be close to zero.

Wayne Lacombe lies awake, Sarah beside him. He should arise and commence with breakfast preparations. He and Sarah are the guides on this international exchange student orientation trip. He gently nudges her and kisses her warm cheek. He wishes they could embrace and lose themselves in the cocoon of their love. But they have landed a contract with the school district and want to make a strong impression on this first outing. The money will help to build the cabin on the piece of river front property they have purchased.

"I'll get the stove started and boil water. You wake the group. See you down at the shelter."

Two tent platforms over, Mahmoud lies still in his thin sleeping bag. He has been dreaming of the White Desert. The cold air reminds him of those nights he spent with his father huddled together behind the windbreak while the wealthy tourists slept in the tents close to the fire.

He rolls over, the slippery sleeping bag sliding across the nylon sleeping mat. The sound awakens his Japanese hiking partner, Shigeru, who rises and mutters, "otoire". The outdoor toilet is some fifty meters away, a shake building with stairs that lead up to a seat suspended over a barrel. Shigeru struggles to unzip his bag and the tent flap, fumbles for his boots and plunges out into the early morning. Mahmoud does not like this toilet and slips behind trees and boulders whenever he needs to relieve himself. His friend, Ahmed, has rigged up an old water bottle to use inside his tent; Mahmoud has done the same, but Shigeru refuses to have such impurity in the same space as his sleeping mat. Mahmoud soon crawls through the flap and out behind the tent; his yellow stream gouges pockets in the wet snow.

This is day two in the Rockies, part of an outdoor adventure camp sponsored by the high school to help foreign students acclimatize. He and Shigeru are among the seven students who left their warm home stays in Vancouver yesterday and made their way by van to this alpine lake. They passed forests of poplar, quickly changing from green to yellow and into higher elevations where stark conifers clung to steep ridges while above them massive dolomite faces towered. Today they will leave the camp and climb higher to view glaciers named after English explorers.

Mahmoud looks up through the trees. Glimpses of rock can be seen as low cloud shifts around the valley. He must move quickly to the cook shelter. He is on the breakfast crew and does not want to upset Wayne, the leader. Mahmoud longs for hot *shai, foull* and fresh *baladi* but knows the menu offers only porridge and hot chocolate.

Sarah and Wayne work in tandem to engage and motivate the young people under their charge. Their outdoor experiences together have rendered them compatible in all settings and conditions. Each takes cues from the other, resulting in a harmony of practiced teamwork. In short order, the breakfast crew eats while the clean up crew has already begun the dishes. Sarah and Wayne quickly load first aid gear and lunch supplies. It's too cold this morning to be sitting around. They both know they need to keep this group of novices moving.

Shigeru, alone at the end of the picnic table, is slurping noodles and sipping green tea, much to the frustration of Mahmoud who has dutifully downed his oatmeal and overly sweet hot chocolate. Shigeru, it appears, has packed his own meals and just adds water to clearly marked plastic zip lock bags which he is now neatly repacking into his sealed food bag. Shigeru fashions all the latest camping technology, from his gortex boots to his rainproof head covering, even a water resistant map case. Mahmoud watches him slowly filter enough water for his camel pack; Shigeru does not draw from the communal water pot that Wayne has been boiling since six thirty.

Shigeru lifts his head and nods. "Ohio!"

"Massa el khahir!"

Wayne interrupts their morning salutations.

"Ten minutes until departure and remember, you guys, English only today."

He stares, good humouredly at Shigeru and Mahmoud. An important aspect of the school contract is English conversation. An ESOL instructor from one of the high schools was scheduled to accompany them on this outing but pulled out because of a serious illness in her family. No one else could be secured at such a late date. Not wanting to lose this opportunity to demonstrate their skills, Wayne and Sarah assured the administration that they would engage every student each day. They would promote journal entries and include writing time during their evening programme. This is the first of what they hope will be many contracts with the school district. Outdoor education is a buzz word, at present, and they want to establish themselves early as leaders in this new field. Perhaps school trips could become a new career for both of them. On this they speak with one voice.

The trail starts in the trees just behind the camp. The slow convoy, led by Sarah, hits the first major elevation change as the cold rain changes to large sloppy flakes. Small rivulets race down the muddy incline and are held by slippery roots that need to be avoided to ensure a firm footing. Many of the novice hikers stumble and slide as they scramble to keep up with Sarah's challenging pace.

Wayne, at the rear, shouts up ahead.

"Hey Sarah, slow it down a little will you? We have another five hours of this!"

Shigeru faintly detects moans of displeasure from the two girls in front of him. Since crossing the last creek he has focused his eyes on the shapely buttocks of the Swedish girl, Ilse, as the corduroy stretched and slackened with each of her steps upward. This was how he managed to survive those endurance runs with the cross country club back home. He would select a fast female runner to shadow, being pulled along by the undulations of her firm behind - some slipstream! Now Juanita is in front of him. Less fit and less agile, she continually places her feet on the treacherous roots that cause her to topple, releasing language of questionable origin.

He mentally recalls the well-groomed hiking trails in the Rokko Mountains near his home in Kobe, where he and the rest of the outdoor club spent most of their weekends. Many of the steep sections boasted carved steps of rock and concrete. At the end of these walks, a hot *ofuro* awaited, with the promise of glimpsing his scantily clad female classmates in their after bath *ukata*.

These visions soon disappear as he runs head long into the rear end of Juanita who has bent down in front of him to tie her bootlace.

"Gomen nasai," he quickly apologizes.

"No problem. I borrowed my home stay sister's boots and they just don't fit very well. This is steep, isn't it? I guess I'm not in very good shape."

Juanita reaches into the top of her pack, pulls out a blue tube, puts it to her mouth and takes in a deep breath.

"Ah...So, desuka!"

Juanita is overweight in Shigeru's mind, but everyone here seems to be overweight. On arrival at the Vancouver airport he was shocked at the size of everyone in the McDonalds, hunched over boxes of greasy fries and super sized milkshakes. He longs for the slim hipped girls he hung out with at Motomachi after *juku* in the evenings. He doesn't know where Juanita is from, but her English is the envy of all the new students. He thinks maybe she is Spanish or Portuguese.

"Let's helping...me and you."

Shigeru works his broken English as he holds up Juanita's yellow daypack so she can slip the straps over her shoulder.

She smiles, gives him a short bow, and continues to place one oversized boot in front of the other up the trail.

At Douglas Lake the crew takes a break. Sarah and Wayne pass out granola bars and dried banana chips. Everyone is reminded to drink frequently as they are losing much water from perspiration. Some quips are made by the girls about losing weight too.

Wayne and Sarah discuss the weather and trail conditions. The forecast calls for clearing in the late morning and sunshine the rest of the day. They have chosen a tough trail for the first day but are familiar with its challenge. They know the trail well, having walked it several times with friends last spring but the unexpected snow has made conditions more difficult than they would like. Sarah considers turning back but Wayne assures her that the ceiling is lifting and by the time they reach the glacier they will be surrounded by blue.

Mahmoud leaves Ahmed and sidles up to Juanita who offers him half of her granola bar. He has been watching her since the first day of orientation. She reminds him of the full-bodied girls at the oasis but shows none of the signs of shyness, which is the custom of Egyptian women. She is friendly and he recalls her cushioned hug after a dinner gathering at the high school. She seems to know that he is homesick.

He wonders about his decision to come here, not that it was his decision. His father had wanted it. His father, who made good money guiding foreigners deep into the Great Sand Sea and on to the Cave of Swimmers, wanted a son who could speak more English than he, better English than he. When a Canadian teacher and his family had befriended Ashraf, his father, after many desert trips together, he offered Mahmoud a year in their home in Vancouver. The arrangement was made; Mahmoud was informed later.

"But I don't want to leave the oasis, he pleaded. I am Arab; I belong here. I will make my future in the desert, *inshallah!*"

"You will obey your father!"

At first, the novelty of living in Canada for a year made him a celebrity in Bahariya. He was leaving the oasis to live in the West, the unknown west, the evil west, according to some in the village. He was told to beware of temptations, read the Koran, and to remember his family. His father had high expectations. To become fluent in English, to come back and become a partner in the touring company and to entice more foreigners with his advanced English skills. After two weeks in Canada he was beginning to have some doubts.

In Canada, he felt exposed, something he had never experienced in the desert, in spite of its endless horizon. In Canada, he was the subject of constant observation, suspicious observation. He was scrutinized everywhere he went with his host family. He was not deaf to the anti Arab whisperings; even the word "terrorist" had stung his ears on one occasion. Lost in a crowd of hostile strangers, Mahmoud continually pondered Allah's purpose of placing him in this wilderness.

Meeting Ahmed from Saudi had been a godsend. At least they could converse together in Arabic. Ahmed was the grandson of some prince and they had little in common other than their faith. He and Ahmed would steal away at sunset and face Mecca together remembering their homelands.

The break is over, backpacks are lifted from the damp ground and the slow shuffles move away from the lake. The sleet has stopped and the visibility is improving. The trail zigzags its way up the side of a cliff until it reaches a natural promontory. "Pulpit rock" proclaims the soggy map that Wayne is sharing with those closest to him. Sarah proceeds to name the peaks that surrounded them, some partially visible, others obscured by low cloud.

Juanita pulls binoculars from her backpack and holds them up to Shigeru.

"Here Shiggy, take a look while I drink some water."

Her smile is a small offering.

"I'm sorry to have held you up on the trail."

"In behind that ridge is the glacier," Sarah informs the group.

Everyone strains northwest hoping to glimpse something of their goal. Suddenly the clouds lift up and the blue white gleam of ice can be detected. Voices of awe echo from the rock face behind them. And as fast as the glacier has appeared it vanishes into the cloud.

The journey now takes them across the face of sharp bluffs, the trail barely clinging to the side of the mountain. Above loom steep snow-covered cliffs that are dripping water as the daytime temperatures move above zero. Below them, loose rock continues on a critical angle for several hundred feet to a ledge and then straight down to the lake.

"Don't look down unless you have come to a complete stop," warns Wayne. "Keep your eyes on the trail."

Juanita, usually the chatterbox, has become very quiet as she negotiates each rock on the thin ribbon that lies before them. Mahmoud can hear Juanita's forced breathing behind him but does not want to jeopardize his balance by turning around to check on her. Besides, everyone's life is in Allah's hands.

Shigeru is in his element. He paces with confidence, continually looking around taking in the magnificent vistas to his right, left and below. Up ahead he can see rock falling from above, dropping to the bluffs, gathering momentum and other rock as it plummets towards the lake. The delayed sound soon reaches the group and all stop at once to stare.

"We must keep moving through this section," orders Wayne. "This is avalanche country and we don't want to be caught standing in the wrong place at the wrong time."

Shigeru snaps his camera from his fanny pack and shoots a few pictures. The sun is straining to burn off the cloud and the lighting is ethereal. He wants to send a few pics to his family in Kobe in his next email. These would be perfect. His parents had been to the Rockies on their honeymoon; Lake Louise lies right behind the glacier they are headed for today.

"Shiggy," shouts Wayne, "put that camera away and get moving."

"Gomen," he replies and steps forward just as a huge chunk of rock released from above topples and slides towards the group in front of him. He and Wayne stop dead as those ahead run forward trying to out speed the gathering rock slide.

Juanita is outdistanced by the rest, her fear and sloppy boots impeding her progress. She looks up and is caught by the leading edge of the slide, lifted off the trail and carried down the cliff towards the lake, yet halts on the precarious ledge below. An orange toque and a yellow backpack can be detected amidst the cairn of death.

A silence pervades the mountain. No one moves. All eyes are trained on the rock pile below. Some crying is audible from the group beyond the impassable chute that separates Shigeru and Wayne from the others.

And then some movement below. A hand struggles to topple loose rock on the surface of the mound. Juanita is alive on the ledge buried beneath the rubble.

Shigeru has visions of his grandmother trapped beneath the heavy roof tiles of her Kitano home after the Great Hanshin earthquake, flames from leaking gas lines quickly approaching. The situation had seemed hopeless; the forces of nature were not to be trifled with.

Sarah takes charge. She shouts across to Wayne.

"Return to the camp! Inform the ranger and bring back ropes and a sling. I'll remain with the group and move to more stable ground. Shigeru, stay where you are and wait."

Wayne gestures a thumbs up and tosses a kiss to Sarah. He turns and departs giving Shiggy a pat on the shoulder.

"It's going to be OK!"

It would be at least an hour before he would reach the lodge at the lake.

A few moments, then Sarah is barking orders across to Shigeru.

"Take off your pack and try to make your way down to the ledge. You have better footing than we have over here. Use those larger rocks as stepping stones."

Shigeru gingerly unslings his daypack, removing his first aid kit from the side pocket.

And then, another explosion from above and tons of material falls away in slow motion cascading towards the remainder of the hikers who stand in shock, gazing at the pile of mountain that holds Juanita in its grip. Mahmoud, quick on his feet, turns, shouts and launches himself just out of range of this second avalanche. The other five bodies flail in the oncoming storm of rock and snow like coloured berries in a blender.

Mahmoud's eyes follow the melange of packs and rain jackets, rocks and snow over the edge and down as far as his position allows him to see. And then his eyes find those of Shigeru across the abyss.

"We must go off the mountain quick. We will be next. We should not have come here," he whines, almost out of control.

Shigeru pauses. He too wants to leave. But the face of his grandmother cannot be erased from his mind. The small shattered glasses surrounded by ripples of wrinkles. This is a second chance. He might be able to help this time.

"We here stay, Mahmoud. Ano, we helpingu Juanita," he fumbles.

"No," returns Mahmoud. "It is the will of Allah. Juanita must die. It is her time, just as it was the time for Sarah and the others. It is the way of the desert. We cannot interfere in Allah's plan. I am going! Yella bina!"

Mahmoud turns slowly away from the slide and leaning into the cliff moves beyond the chute.

"No. Juanita wa libingu," Shigeru calls after him. "She is living still. Onegaishimasu. Pruesu harup!"

But Mahmoud has disappeared around the next bluff heading for who knows where.

Then Shigeru remembers the thin cord he has in the bottom of his pack, a clothesline he always carries to dry his towel and wet clothing. It might be strong enough to give him some balance as he descends to the rock pile that holds the body of Juanita. If only he could remove some of the boulders before Wayne returned with a rescue team, she might have a chance of survival.

After tying the poly rope to a solid rock he carefully lowers himself one step at a time as Sarah had suggested. He can still hear her voice, emphatic and knowledgeable, surging from that small face surrounded in red curls. And now she is gone. How will Wayne react when he finally returns to find everyone gone, even his confident Sarah.

In less time than he thought, he stands on the ledge with the mucky pile of rock before him.

He shouts the name of Juanita several times and is encouraged to hear a faint murmur in response. Good, she has enough air to breathe, he presumes. The urgency of the situation, however, does not allow him the time or energy to formulate English phrases and he breaks into continuous streams of Japanese, reassuring Juanita that he has come to help, that others are on their way, she needs to hold on. He will pull the rocks away gently and free her body from the mountain.

"Ki o tsukete, Juanita chan. Chotto matte kudasai. Wayne sama wa modorimasu. Matte, matte."

It is at least thirty minutes before he dislodges her right arm and head. Her hair is matted to her face with blood and mud. Her eyes are caked shut. He carefully washes the lacerated skin with his soaked neckerchief and holds the water bottle to her lips. She manages to take in some water and speaks for the first time.

"Inhaler," she whispers, but Shigeru does not understand what she is saying.

"Inhaler," she repeats. "Asthma - can't breathe."

Her breathing is forced, rattled from her chest and wheezed from between her lips. Shigeru thinks that she must have crushed her lungs in the fall and then he remembers the blue tube he had seen her use earlier in the day.

"*Zensoku*," he speaks aloud. The breathing sickness, that his friend Taizo would get every November, when the damp winds blew down from Maya-san.

Her pack had been ripped from her shoulders during the fall and lies not far from the top of the rock pile. Shigeru rescues it easily, unzips the top pouch and removes the blue tube. He has no idea what to do with it. He holds it to Juanita's lips hoping she will suck in whatever the tube contains to help her breathe. But nothing happens. He examines the tube closer noticing that an inner chamber moves up and down like a piston. When he depresses the chamber, a puff of spray emerges from the mouthpiece of the tube. Realizing how the tube operates, Shigeru again places the tube in Juanita's mouth and commences pumping the inner chamber. Three pumps should be enough he imagines, not completely understanding how the tube interacts with the lips.

Several minutes later Juanita seems to be breathing easier and Shigeru proceeds to remove more debris that entraps her body. When the entire rock pile seems to shift as he tries to pry some of the larger boulders out of the way, he stops. He does not want to send the two of them over the edge, and besides, he is tired.

He removes some rice crackers from his fanny pack and chews, the crunch in the silence reminds him that he is alone.

Juanita seems to be asleep. She is breathing but does not respond to his voice or to his touch. He feels helpless. What more can he do? Where is Wayne? How much longer?

The late afternoon shadows created by the looming peaks above stretch across the bluff and the cool air soon follows. Darkness would soon replace the shadows and Shigeru fears the added difficulties the lack of light will bring. He has been in the mountains at night before. But the city was never too far away. Sitting on a cliff on Rokko-san he could see the lights of Kobe below stretching for miles along the coast. Here he can only make out one light that is the lodge where he hopes Wayne has arrived and has secured the help he needs.

The silence is deafening. He needs to keep himself focused. He needs to talk to Juanita and so he starts to tell the story of the earthquake. He hopes she can hear the concern in his voice even though she cannot understand his language.

"I had been asleep at 5:46 on the morning of January 17th. The violent surging of my bed, first sideways then up and down, lasted only twenty seconds but in that short time much of the modern city was reduced to rubble. Thousands lay dying, pinned beneath their homes. At first light my father and I had taken bicycles and made our way to my grandmother's. It was impossible to drive a car; the streets were blocked with fallen buildings. We passed people wandering aimlessly in front of partially collapsed houses not knowing how to begin to search for lost family members and prized possessions. We did not dare to stop, uncertain of Obasan's plight. We crossed an intersection with a car dealer on the corner. A dozen Mercedes sat crushed inside a collapsed showroom. We hurried up the hill pushing our bicycles most of the way and stopped before the wooden gate that marked the entrance to my father's family home. The gate remained standing but most of the house had toppled. We called aloud, 'Obasan'! But there was no response."

"The neighbours, whose house still stood, joined us in trying to remove some of the timbers from the front door. It was then that we heard the first sounds coming from the kitchen in the back of the house. My grandmother had been awake before the earthquake and was preparing breakfast in the kitchen when the first jolts had struck. After negotiating our way around the house through the well tended garden and approaching the barred kitchen window, we could faintly make out her shape trapped under fallen shelves inside the fallen house."

"We worked all morning calling encouraging words to her while trying to dislodge roof tiles and beams. By mid morning the fires had started; leaking gas lines had been ignited by loose electrical wires that were strewn across the streets and into yards. Towards noon, firemen arrived. Houses were burning up and down the street. The neighbour's home that had survived the quake now stood ablaze. Soon my grandmother's home, too, was on fire."

" *Shoganai!*' the fireman had uttered to my father and pushed us back from the house, now engulfed in flames. 'There's nothing to be done!' "

"We turned away, no longer able to offer false hope to my grandmother. Within minutes, the house was consumed by fire. We stood in silent prayer unable to speak to each other."

" 'All is suffering,' the priest reminded us at the funeral. There had been many funerals that January, over five thousand, and in each emotionless ceremony, the message had been the same. We are born into this world of suffering and then we die. We must accept suffering with stiff resolve and no regrets. This lesson remains etched on my heart, carved by a culture of acceptance. 'Shoganai', I keep hearing. There is nothing that can be done."

"And so I sit here looking at you, Juanita. You are my grandmother returned. I will not abandon you to the forces of nature. I will not accept this accident without some resistance."

Shigeru holds her hand and in the approaching darkness he thinks he can detect a faint smile on Juanita's face.

He would tell the story many times, first on the phone to his parents, later to newspaper reporters and broadcasters: the sound of the helicopter, the voices of Wayne and others on the cliff above, the removal of Juanita's inert body from the rocks by search and rescue experts, the warm blankets thrown over him, the hot tea and the hot bath in the motel near the park. And later a thank you note from Juanita's parents in Brazil with a picture of Juanita at the rehab centre smiling. The story also included Mahmoud's rescue from a prospector's shack and his return to the desert and the faith of Allah. But the strongest recollection of all was the face of Wayne Lacombe when the bodies of the others, including Sarah, were recovered from the rubble in the canyon floor. Wayne's silence and ghost like features would haunt Shigeru throughout the remainder of his year in Canada.

1996 - HAPPY CAMP

WAYNE Lacombe stands at the "Scales", peering at the snow face that lies above him. He is burdened with the gear that will sustain him as he climbs over the pass and into the no man's land that lies beyond. There have been others who have gone before, those reckless miners from the winter of 1897 who sacrificed all in pursuit of gold. They too paused here to adjust their loads and to decide what, if anything, they should discard before making the final ascent onto the golden stairs.

Wayne carries more than the forty-five pound pack on his shoulders. Weighing heavy on his mind and heart is the guilt of his fiancée's recent death and the pain runs deep along his spine and into his lower back. This four-day hike was to have been their honeymoon adventure. Today, he does not want to be here, but rather at home brooding with a case of beer at his feet and one in his hand. He is not here alone, however. Joining him now as he ponders life's cruelty is an old friend, the man responsible for dragging him to Alaska, in spite of Wayne's determined resistance.

"It'll be like old times," the voice of Jake Wilson, Wayne's high school confidant and explorer.

"Remember Bryson's history class? We covered all that gold rush stuff. The chekakos going over the Chilkoot Pass, heading for Dawson with the promise of instant wealth. We could walk in their footsteps like we always talked about doing one day."

"And besides, Wayne, you should make this journey... for Sarah."

For Sarah: her quick smile and soft touch leap instantly to Wayne's memory. She remains alive and immediate. She could be just climbing over the last ridge to join him, pulling an apple or granola bar from her magic blue pack to share with him high above Skagway even as the cool breeze rustles the hair that has escaped from beneath her toque. Sarah should be here.

Jake's good-natured counseling continues.

"And remember that poetry we had to memorize in McIntyre's class? 'Tis better to have loved and lost than...'"

"Knock it off, Jake. I don't want to hear any more. Let's just do the hike and forget the rest."

"Sorry."

Jake's reconnection with Wayne has not been an accident. The timing for this hike is good for Jake, too. His daughter is working her way through university; his wife is encouraging the development of individual interests in anticipation of life after kids. And also there was that mid-life anxiety gnawing in Jake's stomach. It was time to refocus. Reconnecting was an important part of that process. He had followed Wayne's recent calamity in the news and immediately made every effort to meet his old friend with the hope of rekindling the magic that rendered them inseparable back in high school. And so this trip to the North.

Wayne now slips the straps from his shoulders and lowers his pack against a massive stone that bears the remains of some stampeder's cache. Rusty nails, a stovetop, cable and some bleached horse bones. Wayne pulls a granola bar from his side pocket and leans against his pack looking back down the narrow pass.

Three thousand feet below lies Sheep Camp, last night's shelter, the temporary home of seven thousand miners in the winter of 1897, all waiting for the final push over the pass. It's difficult to imagine so many bodies crammed into the tiny basin on the Taiya River. Hotels, brothels, and cafes as well as tents filled the banks on either side almost to the hanging glaciers that clung to higher slopes. Men primarily, men alone, disconnected from loved ones, some longing to return home - most already exhausted from the weary journey that still had miles to go. But the Chilkoot Pass was the toughest section. The boat trip from Seattle was long for sure, but these thirty-three miles from Dyea to Bennett Lake and the beginning of the Yukon River system had to be the most demanding.

Wayne and Jake left Dyea yesterday morning, after a half hour van ride from downtown Skagway. The first seven miles of the trail followed the Taiya River, relatively flat and uneventful. At Canyon City, another major miners' settlement, the trail had taken them up and over the canyon walls with a few glimpses of the old telegraph line that ran from Dyea to Bennett Lake. They had arrived at Sheep Camp tired and mosquito harried. An early dinner, an interpretive talk from the ranger, then bed. Several other campers arrived during dinner. A family from Vancouver, a couple from Michigan and three bubbly Australian girls who laughed continuously while Wayne slipped into sleep following a couple of Tylenol taken with a shot of rum.

Wayne can make out the three Aussies now as he peers down the long draw that leads up to the Scales.

"The Scales," reads Jake from the hiker's guide.

"Known as one of the most wretched spots on the trail. Here many of the stampeders became discouraged, discarded their equipment and turned back."

Wayne recalls the laminated photos shared by the ranger last night around the campfire.

"If you look closely you will find no smiling faces in these photos."

Rows of glum and passionless faces. Small groupings of bearded zombies gaze into the camera with unreadable expressions. Disconnected from the past, uncertain of the future, these lost souls stare up at the long chain of men in front of them waiting to cross over to the other side.

"Of the one hundred thousand that left their homes, only a handful struck it rich."

But those fortune seekers knew nothing of what lay ahead, thinks Wayne. They lived only in the present. Calculating how many trips they would have to make up the staircase before they could move on towards the Yukon.

Wayne recalls how most stampeders made over thirty climbs in order to meet the North West Mounted Police requirement of fifteen hundred pounds of supplies, enough to survive a year in the gold fields. He is somewhat relieved that he will make this climb only once.

He zips up his pack and shoulders the weight, just as the Aussies crest the hill, grinning as if they just drifted in on a parachute. The first to reach him is a lively pixie with red cheeks and a smile that could melt ice.

"Don't look so glum mate, we're almost there. Just think how lucky we are compared to those poor sods who had no clue where they were going. This must be the Scales. You blokes take our photo?"

Wayne slips off his pack and takes the camera from her hand. She grins again and pulls her two hiking mates in close. They all beam with a radiance Wayne finds hard to resist. He finds himself almost smiling behind the lens as he presses the shutter button. A quick return to the photos of the miners; these are different times.

"Thanks, I'm Andy, and this is Muriel and Lori and you're?"

"I'm Wayne and this is Jake."

He passes back the camera.

"Where you from?"

"New Zealand."

"Oh, I thought you were Aussies. Sorry. I guess that's like mistaking Canadians for Americans. I just heard the accent and assumed."

"No problem mate, we get that all the time. We're working in Seattle for the year and wanted some adventure before we returned home next month. You guys been in Alaska long?"

Wayne is reluctant to tell his story. The less known the better. He shrugs but Jake picks up the narrative.

"Just here to do the trail. Something we promised ourselves back in high school. Life seems to have held us up a little - like about 20 years. Now we're going to complete an old dream. Right, Wayne?"

"Yeah, we best be heading. Looks like some dark cloud moving in over the pass."

"Sure, maybe see you later, Wayne, at Happy Camp."

Andy grins again and turns back to her chums.

Happy Camp, the first reasonable camping spot after the pass, another three hours beyond the summit. Happy Camp. Wayne plays with the irony, unaware of what those miners could find happy about any of this ordeal. There is no happiness as far as he can see other than in the face of the one called Andy. Probably short for Andrea.

He pauses one last time for a look down the long valley and the steep climb he has already completed. He reflects on the meaning of the Scales. Here, miners dropped what they could no longer carry - impediments in their journey, weight that could not be overcome, no matter how many climbs they might attempt. This was the spot where they let it go.

"Just a moment, Jake. I need a minute."

Wayne shuffles across an exposed rock face and around a corner out of the wind. He reaches down his dry fit and removes a thin chain from round his neck. Fastened to the chain is a small ring with a reddish stone of no particular value. Wayne removes the ring and tries to imagine the small hand that it once adorned. But he struggles to revive the flesh that he once held so close. He quickly pulls aside a large piece of granite, sets the ring beneath, then gently replaces the stone.

He pauses.

How quickly his life has changed. Before Sarah, he had lived like some gold seeker drawn on by promises of a better fortune further up the valley. With Sarah, for the first time, he had been truly happy. She had filled his emptiness and healed his wounds. She had sewn the disparate pieces of his fragmented life together. She had erased all the failures and all the feeble attempts at love that had marked his troubled past. Sarah had done all that. Sarah had shown him that digging deep in the earth for the mother lode far outweighed panning the surface for mere flashes of temporary joy.

And now she was gone.

He had been healed and broken hearted in three short years. But he was not the same. He would live with the irony; he would acknowledge forces beyond his control and he would continue to climb.

Wayne pats the stone then kisses the cold surface.

"Thank you, Sarah."

Soon he is back with Jake. The Kiwi women have moved on ahead of them. He flips his pack on to his back feeling a second wind in his lungs.

He moves past more remnants of a struggle that occurred here over a hundred years ago. All that remains of those tortured lives are the soles of boots and random piles of rust. He looks up and settles his eyes on Andy who is leading them toward Happy Camp.

CPSIA information can be obtained at www.ICGtesting.com
Printed in the USA
LVOW11s0725211014

409642LV00003B/90/P